Having My Baby
An Anthology

by

Imari Jade
Daphne Olivier
Tori L. Ridgewood
Joanne Rawson

Imari Jade ~ Daphne Olivier ~ Tori L. Ridgewood ~ Joanne Rawson

Published by
Melange Books, LLC
White Bear Lake, MN 55110
www.melange-books.com

The Family Plan ~ Copyright © 2012 by Imari Jade
Rock-a-bye-Baby ~ Copyright © 2012 by Daphne Olivier
Tabitha's Solution ~ Copyright © 2012 by Tori L. Ridgewood
Learner Mum ~ Copyright © 2012 by Joanne Rawson

ISBN: 978-1-61235-525-2 Print
ISBN: 978-1-61235-526-9 Ebook

Cover Art by Caroline Andrus

Having My Baby

The Family Plan ~ Imari Jade
Fashion heiress Emily Bucktell finds herself pregnant for haute couture designer Bekim Lacolmn, a man who has a string of girlfriends and is a gigolo like her father. Will the two of them ever get together and form a family? Emily isn't holding her breath.

Rock-a-bye-Baby ~ Daphne Olivier
Wouldn't it be wonderful to know, with absolute certainty, that the baby you're expecting will be perfect in every way? In a future world where parents take this for granted, what could possibly go wrong?

Tabitha's Solution~ Tori L. Ridgewood
Tabitha has had the perfect pregnancy. She wants a perfect birth: all natural, with midwives, in the hospital (just in case). Her supportive husband Alex is by her side. So why does everything else have to go wrong?

Learner Mum ~ Joanne Rawson
Polly Wilkins is a successful freelance journalist slash writer. She has been living with her partner Steve in what her parents call sin for the last eight years. But, to her parent's disappointment, there are no signs of wedding bells or the patter of tiny feet on the horizon. Why? Because Polly, is not in the least bit maternal. Can this all change after Polly and Steve have a torrid weekend looking after her nephew? Or will Polly stick to her guns and loose Steve forever?

Imari Jade ~ Daphne Olivier ~ Tori L. Ridgewood ~ Joanne Rawson

Having My Baby

Imari Jade ~ Daphne Olivier ~ Tori L. Ridgewood ~ Joanne Rawson

The Family Plan

by

Imari Jade

Having My Baby

The Family Plan
Imari Jade

Chapter One

"Where the hell am I?" Emily asked aloud as she woke up with a groan. One pain shot through her head at the same time one shot through her groin. She groaned again, finally opening her eyes. Emily focused on the ceiling fan overhead. Now how did my bra get up there? She sat up. The room spent around her. The sheets slid down and the air from the ceiling fan chilled her. Ooh, I'm naked. How'd that happen?"

Emily pushed the covers aside and stepped off the bed. Ooh, bad move. The room SPUN around her again and her stomach and head protested. Emily grabbed hold of the Paul Bunyan bedpost just as a wave of dizziness overtook her. Oh, that's right. The company's annual Fourth of July picnic.

She looked down. The rest of her clothes lay scattered on the floor. What's this? A tie? Emily stooped down and picked the tie up. Why does my butt feel sticky? She examined the tie. It was made of Italian silk. Nice taste. Who does it belong to? She tossed the tie on the dresser on her way to the bathroom. My thighs feel sticky too.

Emily turned on the light in the bathroom, looked down at her body and screamed. "Oh lord I've had sex with someone!"

Emily climbed into the tub after the hysterics died away. She tried to recall the events of last night while she soaked in the warm sudsy water.

She scrubbed her body furiously to wash away the shame. She remembered arriving at the picnic with her best friend Deandria. There was some drinking and toasting, and then more drinking and toasting. Somewhere around midnight she remembered watching the fireworks display with someone. A man. There had been some hugging and more drinking and toasting. Oh my gawd, Bekim Lacolmn. Not him. Please not him.

Bekim was one of her company's clothing designers, and notoriously known throughout the design world for his womanizing ways. Had she spent the night with him? Emily felt a gag coming on. He was everything she hated in a man. No, I don't even like him.

Emily got out the tub and walked into the bedroom and picked up the tie again. It smelt of cologne, Bekim's. Emily got a flashback and dropped the tie like it was on fire. Bekim does have a tie like that. She remembered admiring it once. He had such impeccable style when it came to clothing. Don't panic. Maybe he won't remember anything either.

Emily got dressed. She wouldn't know anything until tomorrow when she returned to work. She stripped the dirty linen from the bed and took them downstairs to wash. Her legs trembled when the events of last night began to play back in her mind. She hurried back up the stairs to the bathroom to look for an antacid to soothe her nervous stomach.

* * * *

Tuesday arrived quicker than Emily expected. It took her a day to get over the yucky feeling from drinking too much, and now she just had to deal with the fright of having to face Bekim. Emily made a mental note never to drink beer ever again.

Emily prided herself on her cool head and rational choice of dating. She'd never had a one-night stand in her life and she didn't know how to deal with it. What was she supposed to say to him? Thanks for the sex? Hell, she didn't even remember it. But her body still felt sore. Apparently she'd used some muscles she hadn't used in a long time. In this sentence you used the word used twice. Can it be rewritten?

Did he use protection? Panic set in again. She sure as hell hoped so. She couldn't use the pill and her system rejected almost everything the gynecologist had suggested. Emily hadn't been with a man in years, but she kept a supply of condoms in her night table drawer just to be on the safe side. She groaned. Bekim didn't seem like the type to pry, so he probably didn't open the drawer. As many women as he'd messed with she hoped he had common sense to have stock in a condom company and a big supply in his wallet.

Emily left the house and took the subway to the building where she worked. There were a lot of cars and foot traffic, she discovered as she walked down Thirty-Fourth Street, which catered to all aspects of the fashion industry. She'd walked the same path five or six days a week for the last seventeen years since she came to New York to live with her father after her mother died.

Emily dodged a rack of clothing as two guys pulled them away from the curb and tried to maneuver it into one of the fashion showrooms. This was also a normal sight in the Garment District of Manhattan. Every day one could see delivery trucks, the sidewalks lined with clothing, frantic designers and bitchy models.

Emily finally arrived at the House of Bucktell where she'd been working since she turned sixteen. Her father, Solomon, was the CEO and had allowed her to work her way up, making sure she learned every aspect of the business from how to sort the incoming mail, cutting patterns and choosing fabrics by texture and color. She apprenticed for him during that time. Solomon was a loving and caring father at home, but a very strict boss who insisted on no less than perfection. Seventeen years later he was still that way. She continued to help out in the mail room every now and then, but her current position of head technical designer kept her very busy.

Emily entered the building and took the elevator up to the thirty-second floor where the House of Bucktell's administrations office resided. The actual production side of the business was located just one floor below, but most of the think work happened on the administrative floor.

"Good morning, Miss Bucktell," one of the administrative clerks said to Emily as she walked through the door.

"Good morning, Jasmin." Emily made a point to learn each and every employee's name. The House of Bucktell stayed on top of the fashion world because of its excellent creations and their friendly atmosphere it provided for its employees. Emily wasn't much of a socializer. In fact, the recent Fourth of July picnic was the first company-sponsored event she'd attended in years. But she wasn't there to make friends. Her job was to supervise production of an outfit from inception to rack. She didn't have time to make friends, not when she had to appease designer's egos and keep spoiled models in line.

The nighttime cleaning crew were just wrapping up. Emily passed several workers moving vacuum cleaners and pushing cleaning supply carts to the maintenance room. A window washer waved to her from outside one of the huge window. Emily waved back. The administrative floor had recently been remodeled and two contractors were busy hanging a huge round pink and brown emblem on one of the lobby walls. The sign had a capital "B" brightly embossed in gold in the center of the emblem. Bucktell had been in business for sixty years and the name was synonymous for fine clothing and accessories. Her grandfather, the original owner, died a couple of years ago, but her father carried the reign of boss with honor. She left the administration lobby and walked down the brown-carpeted hall to Solomon's office. She found him, as expected, with his head buried in a French newspaper, checking out the latest fashions.

Solomon met her Alabama-born fashion consultant mother, Erica in Paris. They married a year before Emily was born and were divorced two years later when it became common knowledge Solomon Bucktell had a mistress. Erica took baby Emily back to Alabama where she managed a successful consultant business until her death eighteen years ago. Fourteen-year-old Emily arrived at her father's mansion dressed in black mourning wear. Emily was tall for her age and already had a sense of style. Solomon took one look at her, cried and then welcomed her with open arms. He also stuck her in her first fashion show shortly after that because she was tall for her age and had a slender build. Of course it took Emily some time to warm up to her father. The same went for whatever woman he dated at the time. There had been so many women in his life she'd lost count. Emily loved her father, but she'd never marry a man with his thirst for women.

Solomon looked up. "Oh, Emily, darling, you're here. Come on in."

At sixty, Solomon Bucktell could still be considered handsome, with his full head of thick silver gray hair, a well-groomed mustache and goatee, and a fit body he kept toned by visiting the gym regularly.

"Is that a new suit?" he asked.

"Yes," Emily said, modeling the navy blue pinstriped suit, Shane, one of their resident designers created for her. At thirty-two, Emily stood five feet ten inches tall and still had a slim build. She was heavier at the

Imari Jade ~ Daphne Olivier ~ Tori L. Ridgewood ~ Joanne Rawson

top and hips than she was when she first arrived at the House of Bucktell, but she still maintained a decent weight. "Shane designed it for me."

"It's very nice," Solomon said. "Maybe you'll pick yourself up a husband today."

Emily rolled her eyes at him and sat down, crossing her long legs before her. He'd been trying to marry her off since her eighteenth birthday. She'd received plenty of offers, but Emily just wasn't interested in settling down and starting a family. She loved her job, but raising babies she'd leave to other women. "Don't hold your breath," she told him.

"I don't understand why you're so against settling down. You're beautiful, intelligent and you'd make some man a fine wife."

"I just don't want to be just some man's wife. I like my job and I don't have to answer to anyone."

Solomon chuckled. "You remind me so much of your mother. She had that same attitude, but I eventually wore her down."

"Don't go there," Emily said. At thirty-two she was old enough to speak frankly with her father. "You cheated on her."

"That doesn't mean I didn't love her. How could I not love her? She gave me you."

"Yes, well," Emily said, straightening out the tailored-to-fit blazer. "I'm still waiting for some sibling to appear demanding his or her place in your heart and a share of the business."

Solomon chuckled again. "You don't have to worry about that. I might have been a lousy husband, but I did practice safe sex."

Emily grimaced. She couldn't do anything about what happened in the past, but she didn't need to hear about it. "How's the fashions in Paris these days?" she asked, changing the subject.

"Interesting," Solomon said, looking down at his newspaper. "The models are getting plumper and the designers are going wild using color combinations you'd never dream of using together."

"I'll check it out in a couple of months when I go there," Emily said. She had signed on to attend a conference there and looked forward to hobnobbing with some of her old friends.

"You might think about taking Bekim along with you. He's always wanted to see Paris."

Emily scowled. Bekim Lacolmn was Bucktell's senior fashion

12

designer, who also apprenticed with her father. Solomon loved Bekim like a son, and even though they didn't share blood, Bekim inherited a lot of her father's habits. At thirty-five, the tall and handsome designer never lacked female companionship. It was normal to see some model draped on Bekim's arm or some rising young starlet seated in his office discussing their date or his plan to design a line of clothing exclusively for her.

She and Bekim got along like fire and water. She respected him as a designer, but hated everything he stood for as a man. "No thanks," Emily said. "This is a working conference. I won't have time to baby-sit the resident gigolo."

"Ouch," Solomon said. "I thought that was my moniker. Bekim's really not that bad. He can't help it if women gravitate toward him. And you have to admit he's a fantastic designer."

True, she could admit that.

"And he's quite handsome."

True. Mother Nature had been very generous with Bekim. She conjured up his image. Bekim stood five feet, eleven, and weighing possible one hundred and seventy-five pounds. He had a great build and he did do a stunt as a model in his youth. He kept the physique by hanging out at the gym with her father. He also had the nicest thick jet-black hair. And like her father, he sported a well-groomed mustache and goatee, which gave his face personality and made those ice-blue eyes pop. Emily shook the image away. She so didn't want to think of him after what had occurred between them two nights ago. Good thing for her she'd been too drunk to remember. "I'll think about it," she said to get her father to stop mentioning Bekim. She planned to avoid the designer like the plague today and possibly for the rest of the week until the little disaster was far behind her. Emily rose. "I better get to work. The rest of the employees should be in shortly."

"Oh, I almost forgot," Solomon said. "Bucktell has been asked to create a fall/winter Young Adult line for Niemeyer's."

"What?" Emily asked almost falling off her three-inch heels. "When did you find this out?" Niemeyer's was a major chain of department stores around the country.

"A couple of days ago," Solomon answered.

"But that only gives us two months to design and deliver," Emily protested.

"And?" Solomon asked. "You've worked against deadlines before."

"Not intentionally," Emily whined. It took a lot of work to get a specialty line together. Designs had to be created, patterns constructed and cut, fabrics had to be selected and not to mention the number of man-hours it took to get the outfits sewn and finished.

"I'll leave it all in your hands," Solomon said, going back to his newspaper. "I have faith in you."

Emily walked toward the door. "Thanks," she said. Her mind spent a mile a minute. "Ah hell, Shane's still in the hospital. Who am I going to get to design this line?"

Shane had taken a nasty fall last week while riding a dirt bike and had broken both his legs.

"Ask Bekim," Solomon suggested. "Maybe he can spare a moment or two."

Bekim normally designed haute couture…clothing made especially for an individual. Bekim designed exclusive custom-fit creations made from high-quality expensive fabrics and sewn with extreme attention to detail. Bekim was a perfectionist and in high demand this time of year with the approach of the holidays and Fashion Week. Fashion Week occurred twice a year in New York and around the world. And she knew for a fact Bekim had been busy finalizing his contribution for the September event. "He might be too busy with Fashion Week to help," Emily said.

"You won't know until you ask him. I'm sure he'll agree to do it if you ask him."

"I doubt that. The man hates me."

"You two looked pretty chummy at the picnic the other day," Solomon said. "That was some kiss you laid on him during the firework display."

"What kiss?" Emily asked. "I don't remember kissing him."

"You never could hold your beer," Solomon replied. "You kissed him at midnight. Everyone saw. You two looked quite romantic under a sky of fireworks. You had your legs wrapped around his waist and he was kissing you back passionately."

Emily opened her mouth to protest, but she just stood there gaping in surprised. "No!"

Solomon laughed. "Yes. Quite a few of us captured it on video. I plan to show it to your kids one of these days."

"Arg!" Emily said, stamping out his office. "I'll sue anyone who posts that picture to Facebook."

* * * *

Bekim watched Emily leave her father's office in a huff. He sighed, wondering what had her knickers in a tangle this time. Emily wasn't a typical spoiled American heiress, but she had her moments. She was a perfectionist and liked to get her way. She was also argumentative, anal retentive and opinionated. Also beautiful, talented and a great lay. The latter description set off a thumping in his heart as he remembered their time together the other night. He supposed Emily didn't remember much of it because of the amount of beer she consumed at the picnic, but he hoped she remembered how she trembled in his arms again and again as she climaxed, before dozing off sleep.

He felt like a cad for taking advantage of her in that condition, but he'd been infatuated with the statuesque technical designer since the first time they were introduced, and he couldn't pass up the opportunity after she offered herself to him so nicely.

Emily slammed her office door, jolting him out of the memory. He's been a little more than sober himself, and he'd done something foolish and forgotten to use a condom. Something like that never happened to him before and he was prepared to deal with the consequences. He wouldn't mind having a baby with Emily. They just had to get past the part that she couldn't stand the ground he walked on. Bekim smiled. She did truly deserve the moniker of Dragon Queen, the other employees dubbed her. They'd had their share of arguments over the years, and there was no hiding how she felt about the constant influx of women in his life. He couldn't help it if other women found him desirable. And only a fool would turn down free sex.

Bekim walked down to Solomon's office and knocked on the door before entering. Solomon Bucktell was his mentor as well as his friend. And they often spent time together at and away from the fashion house.

"Come in," Solomon said, looking up from his newspaper. "Emily and I were just discussing you."

Bekim continued into the plush executive office and sat down in one of the two gold, pink and brown upholstered chairs. "Oh, is that why she just stormed out of here?" Bekim asked. Hopefully Emily hadn't discussed their night together with her father. But he was prepared to take full responsibility for his actions. He would even marry Emily and make an honest woman out of her. He frowned. But that would mean he would have to give up Simone, Gizelle, and Camille. He relaxed his face. But Emily Bucktell was indeed worth the sacrifice.

"No, I teased her about the kiss you two shared at the picnic the other night." Solomon chuckled. "She didn't believe it at first, but I think she finally remembers it. She'd only had a couple of beers. Since she doesn't normally drink I think it brought out her inhibitions more."

Bekim straightened his tie and then crossed his legs. "I don't regret kissing her. In fact, I'm rather proud of it. You know how I feel about her."

"Yes, I do know," Solomon said. "I'm pretty proud of you too for seizing the moment. Emily is not the easiest woman in the world to get next to. She reminds me a lot of her mother…fiery and passionate, but a bit of a shrew."

Bekim nodded and smirked.

"One of these days she's going to realized you're perfect for her."

"Yeah, when hell freezes over," Bekim said. "So what were the two of you discussing?"

"The two of you working together on a special project I agreed to do."

"What kind of project?" Bekim asked. He'd been a party to Solomon's last minute special projects before. The older man hardly ever refused work and very seldom listened to employee's complaints about having to juggle other projects to handle it.

"Niemeyer's Department Store wants us to develop a fall/winter Young Adult collection for them."

Bekim glared at him. "But it's July. That would only give us two months."

"I have faith in you," Solomon said, ignoring his concern. "Emily has agreed to work as technical designer if you agree to do the designs."

Hmm, the opportunity to work side by side with the beautiful Dragon Queen. "What's in it for me?"

"I never could put anything over on you. Niemeyer's is paying top dollar and has agreed to let you include your label."

My label on an exclusive design? That sounds tempting. He'd always wanted to design something for the younger generation that didn't involve sewing on lace and sequence. Most of his older clients insisted that he hand sew most of their haute counter wear. "I'm in,"

16

Bekim said. "If you're sure Emily wants me to work with her." Normally she worked with Shane whom she could boss around and wrap around her finger.

"Oh, she wants you," Solomon said. "She just doesn't know it yet."

"We are talking about wanting me as a designer?" Bekim asked. He didn't miss that little conniving twinkle in Solomon's eyes.

"Whatever," Solomon said. "I'm in your corner."

"What happened to blood being thicker than water?" Bekim asked, rising.

"A blood relative will stab you in the back when it comes to business. But a man in love will do anything in his power to please a future father-in-law."

"Oh!" Bekim said, hurrying to the door. *It's a setup. Solomon is attempting matchmaking again.* "Okay, I'll speak with Emily later and get back to you if she doesn't strangle me first."

Solomon's warm chuckle followed him out of the office and into the hall. "Old schemer," Bekim mumbled with a smile. He wasn't opposed to some fatherly help. Bekim looked at his watch. "Egad. Camille will be arriving soon." He made a mad dash to his office before the model arrived.

* * * *

Emily grimaced the moment she heard Camille Davenport's gravely little girl's voice permeating through the office walls once she arrived. Camille was one of Bucktell's highest paid fashion models, as well as one of Bekim's current girlfriends. Camille was tall and thin as a pin, with a mane of red hair and big blue eyes. She had a walk that made men pant, and a voice that made Emily's hair stand on edge. And she could be a bitch with her demands. She had to have a special brand of water when she worked, and only one specific makeup artist could touch her delicate face, and only Bekim could design for her.

"You better wipe that grimace from your face before she comes in here," Deandria Mitchell, Emily's best friend and the House of Bucktell's resident senior pattern maker said to her. Deandria's job was to draft the shape and sizes of the garment pieces by hand or with the aid of computer software.

"Fuck her," Emily said. "The last time I checked this was still my father's company and she was still just an employee."

"She can also be your future mother-in-law if Solomon can pry her away from Bekim."

Emily hissed at Deandria. "Don't even jest."

Deandria chuckled and her dark brown eyes filled with mirth. Deandria's skin tone was like a mixture of caramel and mocha. And she could rock any fashionable hairdo with all that thick black hair. Today she wore it fashionably coiffed in cornrows and Afro puffs.

The door opened and Camille entered dressed in a black A-line dress with a matching black pillbox hat and carrying a small black clutch. She looked liked she'd just stepped from the pages of some 1960's fashion magazine. Emily had to admit only Camille could pull off such a look.

Bekim entered next looking suave in a charcoal gray suit that brought out the sky blue in his eyes. He also sported a fresh new haircut. He normally wore his thick black hair parted to the side with just a bit of bang, but today he'd let the stylist spike up the top and shave it close on the sides. Even his little mustache and goatee looked sexier than normal. "Good morning," he said. "Camille is here for her final fitting."

Camille would be commanding the catwalk in a fashion event on the weekend for the House of Bucktell, along with about twenty-five other models.

"The clothing is waiting for her in the dressing room," Emily said pointing toward the door.

Camille unglued her arm from Bekim's and passed by her, giving her the evil eye.

Emily ignored her too used to Camille's childish antics.

Bekim lifted his eyes to the ceiling and shook his head.

"So, I heard you two are teaming up for another one of Solomon's special projects," Deandria said, breaking the silence.

"So I've heard," Bekim said walking over to the pretty lady with the scissors in her hand. "I'm looking forward to it if all parties agree to allow me to be the designer." He looked over at her.

Emily rolled her eyes at him. "I have no problems working with you as long as you create something sensational and limit your phone calls to the bare minimum." Bekim's cell phone went off all day with calls and text messages.

"I'll turn it to stun," Bekim said.

Emily laughed sarcastically at his joke.

"Or vibrate, and keep it in my pants pocket for a little thrill."

"Gross," Emily said, getting the sexual innuendo. She almost commented and then she remembered how she woke up naked and sticky the other morning.

Camille exited the fitting room looking cute in a one-of-a-kind Bekim original. It was a stunning light blue gown embroidered with a dark blue sequence neckline. The color simply brought out the beauty of Camille's face. Camille had swept her long red hair over her left shoulder giving her the appearance of a Greek goddess. Emily frowned on the inside. She bet Camille never woke up with semen drying on her shaved pussy.

Bekim rushed over to the model and positioned her in front of the full-length Cheval mirror. "You look beautiful," he told her.

Emily's frown deepened. She did look like a work of heavenly art.

Deandria cleared her throat.

Emily looked her way.

Deandria had the most envious look in her eyes and a fake smile on her lips. Her friend couldn't stand Camille either, but there was no denying the model looked good in the gown.

"Try on the green one next," Bekim instructed Camille. "It's a show stopper."

Camille's skin turned a dark shade of pink as Bekim spoke to her. "Did you create that one too, Bekim?" Camille asked. She always pronounced the designer's name with heavy inferences on the last part, like *Be-kim* instead of *Bek-im*.

"Yes, sweetheart. The green one has Camille written all over it."

Emily would have stuck her finger in her throat and gagged if it wouldn't have appeared childish. It always infuriated her the way men babied and coddled some women.

Camille slinked into the dressing room to change and Bekim returned to his position next to Deandria's workstation. "Well, do you like the gown?" he asked.

"It was okay," Emily said. "The color is perfect for her."

"Would you like one like it?" Bekim asked. "I could design another for you. Of course I would do it in black and add a little more at the top since you have more cleavage than Camille."

"No thanks," Emily said adjusting her blouse around her breasts. "I'm cool. I prefer something a little less dramatic."

"Like a suit of armor," Deandria said.

Emily nodded. "Complete with a chastity belt."

19

Bekim shuddered with displeasure. "You two can make a designer cry. I'm trying to create an illusion here. Fashion consultants and buyers expect nothing but the best from me."

Camille appeared in an emerald green sleeveless mini-dress that showed off her fantastic legs and bare shoulders. The dress came with a pair of matching short gloves and a beautiful green choker.

Emily gawked. The dress did stun.

"Turn for me, darling," Bekim said to Camille as he walked over to her.

Camille turned, revealing the smooth sidelines of the dress and the way Bekim cut it to accentuate her small waist, narrow hips and schoolgirl firm ass. It was indeed a showstopper with the tiny pleats at the center of the back.

"I'd like one of those in red," Deandria said, rising from her seat to get a better look. "But you'll have to add a little more material to get around my hips and ass."

"You are simply scandalous," Emily told her. "Try not to feed his ego too much."

Bekim chuckled and ignored her comment. "Deandria will be beating men off her if I did her up in a red replica."

"I can handle that," Deandria said. "I can stand to beat off a few men."

"What about you, Emily?" Bekim asked. "Perhaps one in silver lamé to fight off some dragons."

Emily scowled at the designer. She'd heard them refer to her as the Dragon Queen before. "No thanks. I don't need sexy clothes to slay a few dragons. I prefer to conquer them with my mind."

"Don't be foolish," Camille told her while admiring her reflection in the mirror. "Men like their women coiffed, not smart."

"Apparently," Emily said, noting the way Bekim was checking the model out. "But I can't fake stupid, and I don't need to get a man." She walked out of the room, leaving the three of them to bask in their silliness.

* * * *

The door to her office opened around noon and Bekim entered. "She's gone," he said.

"I suppose you're referring to Camille. I could care less. You know I only entertain her because my father likes her."

"She's not so bad," Bekim said, entering the room. "And she does look good in my designs."

"Yes, she does," Emily said, wondering why he was in her office.

"I'm here to talk about Niemeyer's fall/winter line, and to get your true opinion on whether we can pull this off in time. We only have two months and we both have other projects."

"Have a seat," Emily told him from a seat behind her desk. "I have some concerns as well. I have a million things to do to get ready for the holiday season and for September's Fashion Week. But he's my father and my boss so I have to consider his suggestions."

Bekim sat down carefully not to wrinkle his suit. "Well, I've taken on several more clients who demand I create an exclusive line of clothing for them. And some special requests for the upcoming Grammy and Oscar award shows."

Emily knew he didn't say this to brag. She'd seen his appointment book and noticed the names of some famous actresses and singers. "We can both tell him, no way," Emily said.

Bekim chuckled. "I don't know if you've noticed or not, but your father doesn't take the word no, well."

"He does have a bit of a temper," Emily said. "And he likes to get his way."

"Not unlike his charming daughter," Bekim added.

"Don't start an argument," Emily said. "Not after we…"

"After we what?" Bekim asked.

Emily refused to continue.

"Oh, you mean the other night. I was wondering how you would broach the subject."

"I have no idea what you're referring to," Emily lied. She could feint ignorance just as well as he could.

"Maybe you were drunker than I imagined. I'm talking about the time we spent together on the Fourth of July. You do remember don't you? Or would you like me to refresh your memory?" He moved his broad shoulders around. "And you must tell your manicurist to round the tips of your fingernails instead of squaring them off. My back was a bloody mess afterward."

"After what?" Emily asked, toying with him.

"After we screwed," Bekim finally said.

Emily frowned. *So it is true?* She and Bekim did do the nasty. "I

21

don't remember," she said. "We're you any good?"

Bekim groaned. "You do go for the jugular, but I didn't hear you complaining."

Emily felt a slight bit of pity for not remembering. "Did I at least enjoy myself?"

"You came a considerable amount of times, if that's what you're asking."

Emily shrugged. She was normally good for a time or two if the man knew what he was doing.

"The bed was quite a mess when I left. And you were sleeping like a baby."

"How did my bra get on the ceiling fan?" Emily asked.

"You tossed it up there," Bekim told him. "After you did a little strip tease for me. You have some pretty smooth moves for a Dragon Queen."

Emily shook her head. She'd liked to remember, but she couldn't.

"Would it help if I told you it was one of the most memorable nights of my life?" Bekim asked.

"No," Emily said. "You don't have to make me feel better about what happened. I'm a big girl and shouldn't drink beer to try to socialize with others. I'm sorry that I don't remember what happened, but I know you won't speak of it again." She picked up her reading glasses and put them on, and then she reached for a pad of paper and a pen. "Let's get down to business. Who else do you want on this team?"

* * * *

Ooh, she is such an infuriating woman, Bekim said to himself as she rattled on about the design team. And why couldn't she remember their night together? He couldn't believe anyone could get that drunk on just a couple beers. He frowned. Maybe she did remember and was just messing with him. He wasn't bragging but he was built ruggedly enough down below to leave a lasting impression. Emily should have woken up very sore the next morning by the way the two of them went at it. She'd been so tight he'd thought he'd split her when he entered her. He smiled to himself. And talk about wet. Damn, her pussy went off like a gusher, drowning him with her feminine juices each time she came. God, he wasn't lying about his back. Emily had scratched the shit out of him, and it would be some time before he could be seen without a shirt. This put a cramp in his love life. How was he going to explain the claw marks to another woman without causing a riot? Bekim shuddered at the memory of Emily wrapping those shapely legs around his waist and begging for him to thrust deeper. If that's how she responded drunk he couldn't wait to fuck her stone cold sober. Just the thought of her wiggling that fantastic ass at him while she stripped for him set a fire in his loins. Emily Bucktell, AKA Dragon Queen had a cunt designed for loving and he tried his best to brand his label inside her.

"Could you at least try to pay attention," Emily told him.

"Sorry," Bekim said. "I was designing in my mind. I do that some times."

"We might have to call Shane for his input," Emily said. "He's done a few pieces for Niemeyer's. We can do a conference call since he can't come to the office until his legs heal."

"I'll set the call up for tomorrow morning," Bekim said. Shane she liked. He wondered if she slept with him. No, he didn't think so. Emily hadn't been a virgin, but she did feel tight from lack of use. "We'll give him some time to get up and take pain medication and then we'll drop the bomb on him."

"He'll be okay," Emily said. "The bulk of the designing will rest on your shoulders."

Bekim's phone vibrated in his pocket. "Excuse me," he said, sliding it out and looked down at the display. It was a text from his sister Glenda. They were meeting for lunch. He texted her back and put the phone away.

Emily went on speaking like she hadn't noticed. He knew how much the phone calls irritated her.

"That should be all for today. We'll meet in the boardroom tomorrow at nine with the rest of the team. Please try to find time in your busy schedule to sketch up a few designs to show us."

"It's just my sister Glenda. I'm joining her for lunch," Bekim explained.

"Not my business," Emily said, dismissing him.

Bekim rose. What could he do to melt that chunk of ice around Emily's heart? "I'll check in with you later," he said walking through the door. "And it is just a lunch date with my sister. I'm not always draped in models."

"Whatever," Emily said. "I just hope we used protection. I wouldn't want to catch anything."

Bekim was just about to tell her the truth when Emily's phone rang.

He left out the office to give her privacy. He'd tell her later.

Chapter Two

"Oh my gawd," Emily groaned as she checked the calendar. August had come and gone and she hadn't gotten her period. Now it was the first week in September and it still hadn't put in an appearance. And she never skipped a month since becoming a woman. *I have some decisions to make.* But first she needed to schedule an appointment with her gynecologist for an exam and a pregnancy test. She'd know what to do once she got the results. On a brighter note, the team had finished with Niemeyer's clothing and she and the others were scheduled to deliver them to the store in a couple of days.

Emily reached for her phone and telephoned Doctor Kim's office.

The receptionist answered promptly. "Doctor Kim's office. How may I help you?"

"Hello, my name is Emily Bucktell and I'd like to schedule an appointment to see Doctor Kim for a pregnancy test."

"Oh, yes, Miss Bucktell. Let me see if he has any openings." There was a pause and then the receptionist returned to the phone. "He has an opening this morning at nine, if you'd like to come in." What time is she calling him? Most offices don't open much before eight thirty does that give her time to be in by nine?

"I'll be there," Emily said. The sooner she found out the better.

"Okay, see you at nine," the receptionist said.

Emily hung up the phone and then lifted the receiver again to telephone her father to let him know she'd be in later.

Solomon sounded concern, but didn't pry. "Just take your time," he told her. "This place isn't going anywhere."

Two hours later Emily sat stunned and confused on the subway as she traveled from Doctor Kim's office to the House of Bucktell's. *Pregnant*. She shuddered. *What am I going to do*?

Emily got off at her stop and walked up the stairs that led to the sidewalk above the subway along with several other riders. A hint of fall was in the air, along with lots of pollution. She walked slowly through the throng of people, considering her options. Emily wasn't keen on the idea of having an abortion, nor did she want to be a single parent. She supposed she should tell Bekim, since it was partially his fault too. But the decision rested solely on her shoulders since it was her body and her choice.

"Good morning, Miss Bucktell," Jasmin said to her.

Emily looked up startled. When did she get to work? She'd been too occupied with her thoughts to pay attention. "Good morning," Emily said. She hadn't seen Bekim until she nearly bumped into him.

"Whoa," he said. "You need to pay attention while wandering through the halls."

Emily looked up at him. "Huh? Oh, I'm sorry. I have something on my mind."

"Anything I can help you with?" he asked.

"No," Emily said absently. "You've done enough."

"Huh?" Bekim asked.

"Never mind," Emily said. "I'm just rambling. Has all the Niemeyer line been brought up from downstairs?"

"Yes, It's in the show room awaiting our final inspection," Bekim said as they walked together away from the administration desk. "Are you sure you're okay? You look a bit pale."

"Pollution," Emily said. "It's very thick outside."

Bekim followed her to the elevator and they entered when it arrived. "I looked at everything earlier. The seamstresses did an excellent job."

Although she valued Bekim's opinion, she'd like to see the work for herself. "What time are the trucks arriving to take the merchandise to Niemeyer's?"

"Noon," Bekim answered. "And shortly afterward I'll be in my office finishing up the stuff for Fashion Week."

Egad, she'd forgotten about that. Shane had sent in his designs and Bekim. And for some reason Bekim was being extra nice and overseeing the work while Shane was home recuperating. And he still had his own designs to worry about.

"Do you need any help?" Emily asked when the elevator door opened.

"Are you offering to assist me?"

Emily glared at him. "Don't make me regret the offer."

Bekim chuckled good-naturedly. "Thanks, but no thanks. I'm almost finished. I've had to cancel some dinner dates and work later than usual to keep up."

"Oh, you poor thing," Emily said sarcastically as she stepped out the elevator.

Bekim followed her to the showroom. She opened the door. Everyone inside stopped what they were doing and then immediately went back to work after recognizing her.

Racks and racks of beautiful fashions in fall colors of green, burnt orange, gold and brown lined the huge room. Garment inspectors checked each item looking for the smallest of flaws before bagging the item.

Emily walked over to one rack and lifted a cute Capri outfit. Bekim had designed it in brown and green with little turned up cuffs at the knees. Emily found herself thinking how cute it would look with a pair of brown wedge sandals and a matching brown canvas bag.

"Well, what do you think?" Bekim asked.

His deep voice broke her train of thought. "It's nice and trendy," Emily said, replacing the outfit back on the rack. "And this is darling," she said lifting a gold short-sleeved minis. The accompanying gold and brown shawl could be used to ward off an evening breeze.

"That would look good on you," Bekim said.

"Yeah, if I was eighteen," Emily replied.

Bekim walked around her. "You still have the figure to pull it off."

Not for long. In about a month or two she'd have a sizable lump just below the navel. That's strange. With my pregnancies, my navel was at the center of the bump. She racked the outfit and walked down the aisle to inspect the men's wear. Bekim had blended the fall colors with dashes of black, rust and green. The male clothing line had a quirky, hip young style with plenty of pockets and would look good on any youth or young man.

There were also some classy dressy fashions in a slightly higher price range. An hour or so later Emily had expected everything and gave it her blessing. She clapped her hands to get everyone's attention. "Okay people, everything looks good. You've done excellent work so get these masterpieces tagged and bagged and moved down to the loading docks so we can meet our noon deadline."

The workers jumped into action, inspecting and bagging the remainder of the merchandise and pushing racks past her and Bekim and out of the door.

Bekim yawned and stretched. "Time for me to get back to work." His cell phone went off.

Emily glared at him. "Keep the call short," she told him, heading toward the door. "Time is money. Fashion Week is a week away." She left the room and headed back to her office.

* * * *

Bekim glanced at the last item in his Fashion Week line, a black and taupe cocktail dress he'd designed for Camille to wear. He'd just put away a silver gown he'd also designed for the model. All the other items, including the men clothing had been tagged, labeled and bagged waiting to taken to the venue where the models would get dressed and perform. *Something is missing.* He turned away trying to conjure up in his mind the correct accessory to be worn with the dress. His creation was gorgeous, but it needed just a little something to make it stand out.

Bekim pulled out a box of costume jewelry he'd designed and began searching through. "Ah," he said pulling out a cameo broach and matching clip-on earrings. *Perfect.* He examined the pieces and carefully wrapped them in tissue and put them inside the bag that contained the dress. He put it away, satisfied with the outcome. Does anyone in fashion really wear clip earrings anymore?

Bekim yawned. He'd put up a good act in front of Emily, but truthfully he felt exhausted and couldn't wait for tonight so he could get some rest. He only had one stop to make after work and then he was homeward bound. He was glad they were able to finish the Niemeyer Collection and he hoped Solomon wouldn't accept any more last minute work for a while. Fashion Week was stressful enough by itself.

"You look tired."

Bekim looked toward the door. Oil heiress, Gizelle Romanoff stood in the doorway looking chic and elegant in a navy blue and white geometrical dress he'd created for her last year. "Gizelle, darling." Had he forgotten a date with her? "Come on in."

They'd met at a party about two years ago. Her father, Nate, owned

28

many oil wells somewhere down in Texas, but he moved the family to New York so Gizelle could get more exposure and probably land her a rich husband.

The raven-haired beauty was well bred and educated, but she was a bit of a wild cat. Gizelle was also the supreme party animal, an A-lister who had no interest in snaring a husband who would interfere with her current lifestyle.

Gizelle walked in carrying a shoulder bag containing Peaches her miniature terrier. Peaches was so small she could fit in the center of his hand, but made this amazing loud yelp when she barked. Right now, thankfully, Peaches snoozed peacefully in her carrier.

Gizelle walked over to a seat and crossed her long legs, giving him a heavenly view of her thighs. "I want to go to Fashion Week, Bekim."

Oh, so this is why she is here. For the last two years she'd wanted the same thing, but both times he had to turn her down because he was busy getting the models ready. Bekim rubbed his temple. "I thought I'd explained it to you before that I will be too busy tending to the models to sit with you in the audience."

Gizelle pouted her peach-tinted lips at him. "But everyone who's anyone will be there. I don't really care if you accompany me or not. I just need to be there."

His manhood would have taken a blow if he weren't used to Gizelle's selfishness. But she wasn't a model, actress or photographer. And this was one of those instances when having money couldn't get you entry. He did have a couple of tickets put aside for fashion magazine editors and reporters, but not for current girlfriends. "So you just want to attend so you'll have something to brag about to your friends."

"Yes," Gizelle said. "Why else would I want to be there? I can care less about what some pencil-thin model is wearing."

Bekim tried to hide his annoyance. Gizelle could be exasperating at times. No, she was a spoiled brat. And she wasn't model material because she was too short and had a voluptuous figure. The twenty-five year old blond would be bored out of her gourd after being at the show five minutes. "I'm sorry, honey. I just can't help you out."

Gizelle leaned forward. "What's it going to take to change your mind? I can make it nice for you." She sounded like a bad Marilyn Monroe impersonator.

Bekim looked her over. Most of her breasts threaten to spill out the dress, which meant she wasn't wearing a bra for support like he'd instructed her when he turned the dress over to her. Still the offer seemed tempting.

Someone cleared a throat in the doorway.

Bekim looked up to find Emily frowning at him. He looked away quickly and over at the breast bearing Gizelle and then back to Emily. Emily had some nice breast too, but right now she had them securely hidden away in a red and bone colored two-pieced suit. He'd bet his last dollar she had on a bra. He turned his attention back on Gizelle. At least he wouldn't have to fight Gizelle to get her into his bed later. "Can I help you, Emily?"

"I just stopped by to see if I could lend you a hand with Shane's collection. But I see you have your hands full."

Emily couldn't stand Gizelle and the feelings were mutual. The two of them had gotten into an argument when Emily walked into Bekim's office and found the young woman half-naked and waiting to surprise him. And of course the Dragon Queen read Gizelle the riot act about it and told her this was a place of business and not a whorehouse. Gizelle hadn't made it any better by telling Emily she was just jealous. He would be sorry to tell Gizelle but she had nothing on the classy Emily Bucktell, except possibly her father had more money than Solomon.

"I'm already finished with both his and mine," Bekim said. "And Gizelle just stopped by to see if I had any tickets to Fashion Week."

Emily gazed over at the heiress. "What's she going to do there? No one will be DJing or passing out gelatin-shots."

Ooh, Emily didn't have to go there. Gizelle might not be perfect, but she did know how to have fun…something Emily should learn to do.

The insult went clear over Gizelle's head. She continued to sit there pouting.

Peaches work up yawned and yelped.

"What is that doing here?" Emily asked. "This isn't a kennel."

Bekim grimaced. Emily didn't even try to be nice.

"I never leave home without Peaches," Gizelle told her. "She gets lonely."

"Well Fashion Week isn't for kids or pets," Emily said. "And it's by invitation only. So if you want to go there you'd better find someone with invitations."

"That's why I'm here," Gizelle said as she glared at Emily.

"Oh, so you thought you could sweet talk Bekim into taking you?" She laughed. "Sorry, honey, he'll be too busy to play with you. He is responsible for dressing several top models like Camille."

"Who's Camille?" Gizelle asked.

"Who's Camille? Bekim, where did you find this one? Camille is one of the hottest models ever to grace the catwalk."

Gizelle still looked puzzled.

"Don't think too hard, honey," Bekim told her. "It doesn't matter."

He looked over at Emily and shook his head at her. Emily had this bemused look on her face. *She can be so petty.*

"I can't take you to Fashion Week, but how about I take you to lunch today?"

"But it's after twelve," Gizelle protested.

"I know a place that serves lunch all day," Bekim told the heiress. He rose from his chair and reached for his jacket.

Gizelle rose. "I hope they let dogs in because I'm not going anywhere without Peaches."

Emily just chuckled and walked away from his door.

"Sure, honey. This place loves dogs."

* * * *

Emily chuckled all the way back to her office until she realized that Bekim was about to go out on a date. She absently touched her stomach as she entered the room. He was making the decision easier for her. But she couldn't think about that right now. She still had so many things to do like make sure all the models knew what they were supposed to wear for Fashion Week, make sure they were available, since some models were in top demand, and she still needed to make appointments to get her hair and nails done. Lastly she had to stop at the drug store to pick up her prescriptions before she went to the grocery.

Bekim returned around two, minus Gizelle and looking very tired. She didn't know how he had time for a personal life when he had so many customers clamoring for his attention. She still hadn't seen his designs for the Grammies, but she was sure they'd be spectacular. Bekim never messed around when it came to work. He was a professional and she expected no less from him.

"I'm back," he said sticking his head into her door.

"How was lunch?"

"Great."

31

"Did Peaches enjoy the ambiance?"

Bekim scowled. "Damn little mutt yapped all through the meal. There was one time I thought we'd be asked to leave. Pets are worse than babies when it comes to enjoying a meal in a restaurant."

Emily tried to keep a straight face. *Is that really how he feels*? "You don't like babies?"

"Who me? Yes, I love babies. But not in restaurants and on planes." He waved to her and continued down the hall to his office.

Emily pushed a button on her keyboard to wake up her monitor and went back to checking her email. There was one message from her doctor reminding her of her next appointment, a couple from some of her old friends, and loads of spam. She got rid of spam, signed out and then surfed over to the company's site on Facebook to answer questions about fashion from some of their fans. Bekim talked her father into opening the account and so far it turned out to be a pretty good idea. Both males and females who just needed a little advice on how to look good for special occasions visited the site frequently.

Next Emily made the appointment for her hair and nails, and then she tackled some of the real mail piling up in her in-basket. There were loads of fashion magazines and books. Most of it belonged to her father, but he insisted she go through the mail for him because he was much too busy. Emily smirked. Yeah right. He was probably on his phone lining up a dinner date for the evening. She couldn't recall the last time he ate at home. She sighed. Maybe the big mansion was a bit lonely now that she'd moved out. She wasn't much of a cook either, but she tried to eat dinner at home five nights out of seven.

After sorting and putting away the mail Emily pulled out a tablet and pen and began composing a grocery list. She needed lots of milk and some fresh fruit and vegetables. And liver. Emily made a face. Doctor Kim said she needed iron and protein, but she hated the heck out of liver. Emily surfed the Internet for a substitute and found oysters and chicken to be good sources. She quickly scratched liver from the list and added oysters and chicken. Then she went to her favorite book-buying site and ordered a book on pregnancy. She'd learn everything she had to just in case she decided to keep the baby. She groaned. She could barely take care of herself.

Emily finished up and then left her office to check on a supply order. Her plans were to leave on time, grocery shop and then go home to take a relaxing bubble bath before turning in for the evening.

* * * *

What were the chances of her running into Bekim in the supermarket? Granted they did live near each other but their paths never crossed before.

"Are you following me?" Bekim asked once he recognized her.

"No, I can barely tolerate you during business hours, so why would I follow you on my free time?"

"Emily, dear, why are you refusing to admit you are infatuated with me?"

Emily turned her nose up at him.

"I'm just teasing." He gazed over into her cart. "Ooh, oysters. Are you expecting company?"

Emily frowned at him. "No, why?"

He pointed to the oysters. "They're supposed to be good for the libido."

"No, only you would use them for that purpose. They're also a healthy source of protein."

"So you're trying to be healthy. I understand. Well, you're giving it a pretty good start with all that milk, chicken and fresh fruit."

Emily gazed over into his basket. He had bottles of wine, cheese and crackers, and a box of condoms. "Are you expecting company?"

"Non!" he said using the French term for no. "I'm just restocking my supply. Dinner tonight will be shrimp and crab fettuccini."

"You can cook?"

"Why would you ask like that? Of course I can cook. I don't go out to dinner with pretty ladies every night like some people assume."

Emily sneered at him. "I just assumed you have someone come in to cook for you. Where are your ingredients?"

"Still on the shelves," Bekim said. "I was just on my way to the seafood counter." He paused. "I have a splendid idea. Why don't you join me for dinner tonight?"

"What? Why?" Emily asked.

"So I can show off my superb culinary skills, and so we can discuss Fashion Week."

She didn't want to have dinner with Bekim and have to be there to hear his phone ringing off the hook. But she really wanted to see his place. She bet the much together designer was a slob at home. No one could be so perfect. He had to have some faults besides being a womanizer. "Okay," she said just to appease her curiosity.

The stunned look on Bekim's face probably meant she shocked him by accepting.

"But I need to finish shopping and go put away my groceries. And I can't stay late because I need my rest."

"Spoken like a true princess. I'll see you in an hour," he told her. "Let me give you the address."

"Don't bother," Emily told him. "I already know."

Bekim raised an eyebrow, but did not comment. "I'll see you soon," he said walking away.

Chapter Three

Emily rode the bus down to Bekim's apartment, got off and walked down the street with throngs of people. Bekim lived in a swanky high-rise building. A doorman allowed her to enter and Emily found the elevator and rode up to the tenth floor. Bekim lived in apartment 1012 at the far end of the hall. She exited the elevator, found the apartment and rang the buzzer. Moments later Bekim opened the door wearing a Kiss the Chef apron along with a pair of gray Armani slacks and a matching short-sleeved pullover shirt.

"You're right on time," he said as he stepped aside and allowed her to enter.

Emily ran her gaze over the hardwood floors and the expensive furniture. Custom made drapes hung from the curtain rods and the place had adequate lighting. "I like everything I see so far."

"Do you also like my apron?" Bekim asked leading her to the kitchen.

"It's very cute," she said as she admired the warm tan and brown colors and the splashes of yellow and green as soon as she stepped through the door. His eye for color and design transcended to his home and she found the place orderly and homey. "Something smells delicious," she said as they entered the kitchen.

"Dinner should be ready in a moment," Bekim said.

"Where can I wash up?"

"The bathroom is down the hall, second door on the right."

Emily walked out the kitchen and found the half-bathroom. There were little duck motifs on the walls and matching accessories like a duck–shaped soap dispenser and ducks on the guest towels.

Emily used the toilet and then washed her hands. She found Bekim stirring a pot when she walked back into the kitchen. Moments later they sat across from each other at a table set intimately for two. He poured a glass of wine for himself but she stuck to bottled water. She sampled the food. "Oh my gawd, this is delicious." The shrimp and crab creation melted on her tongue and the noodles were tender. The cheese sauce didn't overpower the seafood. Halfway through the meal she smelled something sweet. "Are you baking something?"

Bekim nodded. "Dessert. I am preparing a pineapple upside cake."

Emily moaned. "My favorite."

Bekim smirked. "Yes, I know. But if I knew I'd get a response like this from you I would have showered you in cake a long time ago."

Emily smirked and shook her head at him. "I like this side of you."

"What? My witty side?" He made his eyebrows go up and down.

"No, the human side. You seem so relaxed away from the office. And the phone hasn't rung."

Bekim twirled the noodles around on his fork. "I turned my cell phone off. I know you don't like when it rings." He put the tip of the fork in his mouth and sucked at the noodle.

Emily got the shivers just by watching him eat. "I don't like it at work. I can't control what you do on your own time. But thanks for turning it off." She paused. "Oh, wait, what if there's an emergency?"

"I have a house phone," Bekim said after swallowing. "But to tell you the truth I'm not really a fan of the cell phone either. I find it quite annoying to listen to someone's conversation while I'm shopping or on the subway."

Emily nodded. "I find it rude too. Sometimes I like to read a good book on my way to and from work, but I can't concentrate with all the conversations going on around me."

The two of them continued to talk and before she noticed several hours had gone by. They moved from the kitchen to Bekim's design room. She walked over to a rack of clothing. One dress in particular caught her attention immediately. It was a short emerald green after-five. Emily lifted it from the rack to admire it.

"Do you like it?" Bekim asked.

Emily nodded. "I like the color and the beadwork is exquisite. When did you find the time to make something like this with your busy schedule?"

Bekim yawned. "I forgo sleep once or twice a week."

"Poor baby." She actually felt sorry for him.

"Would you like to try it on?"

"It won't fit," Emily said, still running her finger over the beads. "And I don't think Camille would like the idea of me trying on her dress."

"This is not Camille's dress," Bekim said. "You can change behind the screen."

Emily really didn't feel like getting out her clothes after such a delicious meal. All she wanted to do was crawl into a nice comfortable bed and go to sleep. "Okay." She walked toward the screen. "But don't peek." She didn't have on a bra and things were complicated enough between them.

"I wouldn't dream of peeking," Bekim said with a yawn. "I'm too full of cake to budge from this spot."

Emily chuckled as she undressed. She slipped into the dress enjoying the fell of the satin lining. Bekim really knew how to make a woman feel special. Emily tried to zip the zipper, but she couldn't reach it.

"Do you need any help?" Bekim asked.

"I can't zip it."

"Come out and I'll help you."

Emily stepped from behind the screen and nearly walked into Bekim. "I thought you said you couldn't move." Emily turned her back on him.

"Oh my," he said, gawking at her. "You look simply beautiful in this color." He moved the zipper up with ease and then he escorted her over to a full-length mirror so she could see the dress.

"Wow," she said, adjusting the straps on her shoulders. "It looks like it was made for me."

"It was," Bekim said. "I thought you might want something new for the fashion show."

The material molded to every curve. Emily turned around slowly, checking the fit out from the side and back. Her butt looked huge. Emily scowled and tried to pull it in.

"That only works on stomachs," Bekim teased. "Damn, your ass looks bitching."

All the cool brownie points he'd scored this evening flew right out the window. "Unzip me please."

Bekim unzipped slowly and then his hands slid the straps down her arms. He moved his hands to her shoulders and squeezed gently.

A thrill ran through her body as he moved in behind her. "What are you doing?"

"Carpe diem," he said. "I'm seizing the moment." Bekim placed a warm kiss on the back of her neck.

A shudder ran all the way down to her toes. "Don't," she said.

"Too late." Bekim swept her up into his arms and carried her out the room before she could react.

* * * *

No excuses, no alcohol and no clothing. Bekim had the lovely Dragon Queen just where he wanted her...on her back and in his bed. This time he was going to make damn sure she remembered.

Bekim took her time tasting every inch of Emily's shapely body. Her breasts were like two perfect pears with dusty pink nipples. He ran his tongue over both tips until they hardened. He suckled gently on one of them and then moved over to the other.

Emily gasped as he buried his face into her stomach. She had an 'innie'. He tongued her navel and incited a giggle. "That tickles," she said continuing to giggle.

The rare sound warmed his heart and gave him strength to seek out her other treasure. Bekim kissed his way down to her pussy and stopped when the giggling stopped and Emily froze. Bekim lifted Emily's hips and spread her thighs apart. He buried his face between her legs, savoring the sweet delicate aroma of her femininity.

Emily moaned softly.

Bekim sighed inwardly, tired from working so much overtime hours, but determined to give Emily the release she needed. He kissed the lips of her pussy and then rimmed the tiny delicate hole with his tongue.

"Oh!" Emily exclaimed as she tightened her thighs around his head.

Bekim pushed his tongue in further, enjoying the taste of her. He grasped her by both hips and moved her down slowly so he could get more of his tongue inside. After a couple of seconds he removed his tongue and introduced two fingers.

Emily pussy sucked them inside.

Bekim only had to move his fingers in and out of her a couple time before Emily exploded, lifted her butt off the bed and drenched his fingers.

"Oh shit," Emily said. "That was fantastic."

Bekim rose over her. "You ain't seen nothing yet, darling," He rolled over and got a condom out the nightstand. This time there would be no mistakes.

Chapter Four

Two months went by pretty quickly. Fashion Week had come and gone without a hitch and both Bucktell's and Bekim's designs were the hit of the fashion shows. Orders continued to pour in and Solomon was one happy camper with the outcome.

Emily on the other hand, was having a hard time hiding her pregnancy and morning sickness was taking a toll on her. Today a few of them were going out to lunch to celebrate finishing up their work just in time for Thanksgiving. Emily pulled the most concealing outfit she owned from the closet and put it on before leaving for work. She grimaced, knowing she would have to see Bekim today. He hadn't been himself lately since Camille deserted him and hooked up with a guy she met during Fashion Week, and Gizelle was still angry with him for not getting her tickets to the same event.

His cell phone stopped ringing and the two of them never spoke again about the mind-blowing sex they engaged in on the night he cooked her dinner two months ago. She wanted so badly to tell him about the baby then, but couldn't find the words. She'd already made up her mind to keep the baby as soon as she saw her navel protruding. Emily hadn't figured out what she would do or how she was going to raise a baby alone. But right now she just had to get through today.

She barely made it to work before running to her private bathroom to throw up her guts.

Emily spent the rest of the morning in a meeting with her father and some of the senior personnel. Shane had returned to work and she'd been avoiding him for days because he wanted her to try on a dress he'd made for while he was recuperating at home. Emily didn't want to appear rude, but she couldn't undress in front of Shane because he would surely see she was pregnant. Halfway through the meeting she got nauseous again, excused herself and slowly walked out the conference room. She flew to her office, once again barely making it to the toilet. Emily brushed her teeth and garbled and then returned to the meeting.

"Emily, darling, are you okay?" Solomon asked.

Emily nodded. "I'm not feeling well."

"You do look a bit green around the gills. Maybe you should take the rest of the day off."

"I'll be okay," Emily said. "Plus I promised Deandria and the others that I would join them for lunch."

"We can make it some other time," Deandria said.

"Nonsense," Emily replied. "Maybe I'll go lay down in my office for about an hour after the meeting."

"The meeting is dismissed," Solomon said rising. "Go lay down. But if you're not feeling well by noon I'm calling for the car and sending you home."

Emily frowned. He picked a fine time to be a daddy.

Everyone left except Bekim. "Maybe you should listen to Solomon and go home."

"She never listens to anything I say anymore," Solomon said.

"I'm fine," Emily assured them. "I think it was something I ate."

"Or it's the flu," Bekim said reaching up and touching her forehead. "You don't have a fever."

Emily rolled her eyes at him. "I'll be fine by lunch. I don't want to disappoint anyone or have them calling me stuck up." In the past every time she got invited to an office function she found an excuse not to attend.

"They've called you worse," Solomon said.

"You're not funny, Father," Emily said heading toward the door. "I'm going to my office to lie down." She left the two men alone.

"Hold all my calls," Emily said to Jasmin.

"Yes, Miss Bucktell," the receptionist said.

Emily walked past Jasmin and entered her office. Surely the morning sickness would be over soon.

* * * *

"Emily has put on some weight," Shane said to Deandria as the two of them sat in the employee's lounge drinking coffee and eating doughnuts.

"So it's not my imagination," Deandria said.

Shane shook his head. "She's been avoiding me since I returned. I think Emily is embarrassed about it."

"What's Emily embarrassed about?" Bekim asked as he joined them at the table.

"The little weight she's gained," Shane answered.

"Has Emily gained weight?" Bekim asked.

Shane nodded. "Haven't you noticed? Her face if fuller and the suit she's wearing is fitting her snugger than it did when I made it for her."

"Maybe it's her time of the month," Deandria said in her friend's defense. "Women gain weight during this time."

Bekim shook his head. He'd heard similar gossip recently about Emily but he never expected it from her two best friends. "I just think she's sick." He added sugar to his coffee. "But she's too stubborn to go home and rest. Maybe we should cancel lunch."

"Maybe," Shane said, shaking his blond bangs out his eyes. "We'll give her until noon." He laughed. "Maybe she's pregnant."

"Who?" Bekim asked.

"Emily."

"What Emily?" Deandria asked.

"Our Emily," Shane answered.

Deandria laughed this time. "Be serious. Emily isn't dating anyone, and I don't believe she'd be chosen for the next Immaculate Conception because she curses like a sailor."

Shane continued to laugh. "You're so stupid. Maybe she has a man on the side no one knows about."

Bekim raised an eyebrow at Shane's comment. *Emily dating someone, preposterous.* "You too are horrible. Besides what man would subject himself to her fiery temper?"

"You," Shane said as he tore a doughnut apart.

Deandria ignored Shane's statement. "I'm her best friend. She would tell me if she's dating someone. And where would she meet a man anyway? She never goes out."

"That's true," Bekim said. "She's either home or here."

The conversation waned and they went back to eating doughnuts.

Bekim finished his first and rose. "I have to get back to work. I'll see you guys at noon."

42

Deandria and Shane waved to him and Bekim left the lounge and rode the elevator back to his office.

No way, he thought as he slid behind the drafting table. Emily couldn't be pregnant. And the only guys she'd been hanging around lately were him and Solomon. He went back to the design he'd been working on before he stopped for coffee. If Emily were seeing someone, surely Solomon would know.

Emily looked much better when they all assembled in the lobby at noon. The plan was to walk four blocks to Jacoby's Steakhouse for lunch. Jacoby's had the best steaks in the area and Bekim craved beef. He walked and talked with Shane with Emily and Deandria following closely behind. They entered the restaurant and got seated quickly because they had reservations. The steaks arrived and about fifteen minutes into the meal Bekim noticed Emily turning green again.

"Excuse me," she said rising. "I need to use the ladies room." She hurried away before either of them could respond. Ten minutes passed and still she hadn't returned.

Deandria rose. "I'll go check on her."

"Maybe you should since I don't think I can just walk into the ladies room," Shane said.

Bekim smirked at Shane's little joke, but deep inside he worried.

Deandria walked away, leaving him with Shane. Once they left the restaurant he would personally escort Emily home.

* * * *

"Emily, are you okay?" Deandria called out as she entered the ladies room.

"No," Emily moaned. Her stomach rebelled and she vomited again. Emily flushed once the spasms subsided, exited the stall and walked over to the sink.

"You still look green and you're sweating," Deandria said. "I think you have the flu."

Emily pulled a toothbrush and paste from her purse and freshened up her mouth. "It's not the flu," she said once she finished. "I'm pregnant."

Deandria gasped loudly. "What? How? Who?"

"I'm pregnant and you know how." She refused to say his name. The tears slipped from her eyes.

Deandria walked over to her and patted her on the shoulder. "It's

43

going to be okay."

"No it's not. I'm going to have to raise this baby alone and I don't know how."

"What do you mean alone? What about the father?"

"He doesn't know and I don't want him to know."

"Why the hell not?" Deandria asked. "Is he married? Oh gawd don't tell me you've been screwing a married man."

Emily dried her eyes. "No, he's not married, but he's not the fatherly kind. And he's everything I despise in a man."

Deandria chuckled. "Apparently you found something redeeming in him to sleep with him."

"I was drunk and I don't remember much of it."

"No, don't tell me you picked some man up in a bar," Deandria said.

Deandria was getting on her nerves with all the questions.

"No, it happened the night of the company's Fourth of July picnic."

"You met someone at the picnic? When? I was there next to you most of the time except...."

Emily started crying again.

"No!" Deandria said like she discovered the answer and didn't believe her. "Bekim is the father?"

Emily nodded. "So you see why I've been keeping this a secret. The man is a Casanova and a gigolo."

"So is your father honey, but he did okay raising you. And Bekim loves you. Everyone knows this. He's gotten rid of Camille and Gizelle and the two of you would be perfect for each other."

"I think we'd better get back to the table," Emily said drying her eyes for the last time. She reached into her purse, took out her compact and lipstick and repaired her makeup. "Please don't say anything."

Deandria followed her out of the ladies room.

The men had finished their lunch by the time they returned to the table.

"Is everything all right?" Bekim asked Emily as she sat down.

"Yes, thank you. I think I'm going to follow my father's advice and go straight home. I'm still feeling a bit under the weather."

Bekim signaled for the waiter. He paid the bill when the waiter arrived and the four friends walked back to The House of Bucktell.

Solomon called them into his office before Emily had a chance to leave. "I'm glad you're back. I have some wonderful news. The hottest actress in Hollywood, Megan Jefferies wants Bekim to design a line of clothing for her. And I've volunteered the three of you to help him."

Emily was about to open her mouth and protest when she suddenly felt ill again. "That's nice Daddy, but can we discuss this tomorrow? I was just about to go home because I'm still not feeling well."

"But of course, dear. I'll have the car brought to the door," Solomon told her. He went back to discussing his plans with Bekim and the others.

Emily exited her father's office and staggered back to her office holding her stomach. Apparently the morning sickness was going to kill her before she delivered the baby. Emily walked into her private bathroom and threw up again. She pulled out the toothbrush and paste again and freshened up her mouth. She walked back into her office and found Bekim waiting, leaning against her desk. "What are you doing here? I thought I left you with my father." I understand the need for her to freshen up her mouth, but that's three times she's pulled out her toothbrush and toothpaste. We already know her routine, so we don't need to be told over and over again.

"You did, but I got concerned and came to check on you."

Emily walked over to her desk and started packing her things to leave. "I'm okay," she said as she stepped around him. "I just need to lie down." She stepped away from her desk and then she got dizzy. Emily reached for her stomach just as darkness overtook her. "Awe," she groaned just before she passed out.

Emily felt a cool compress on her forehead. She opened her eyes. Bekim glared down at her. "What happened?"

"You passed out," he replied. He seemed concerned. "Are you pregnant?"

Emily sat up quickly. "I don't know what you mean."

"Don't play around. You haven't been yourself for days and everyone's noticed that you've put on a few pounds.

"People are talking about me?"

Bekim nodded.

"Yes," Emily said. "Yes, I'm pregnant, but please don't tell anyone."

Bekim continued to gaze at her.

"What? It's no big deal. Women get pregnant every day." She rose, but still felt dizzy.

"Does your father know?" Bekim asked.

"No. No one knows except you and Deandria. And I would

appreciate if it remains this way."

"But you won't be able to hide it too much longer," Bekim said.

"I'll tell my father later," Emily said, putting her purse in the crook of her arm. "Now I have to leave because I'm sure the driver is getting nervous in front of the building."

Bekim followed her out the office and out to the car. He helped her inside. "I'll call you later to check on you. Try to get some rest."

"I will," Emily said, praying he'd leave before he asked any more questions.

Bekim closed the door and the driver drove away from the curb.

Emily fought to keep the tears from falling. Why did he have to be such a caring bastard?

* * * *

Solomon couldn't stop laughing.

"I don't see why you're laughing," Emily said. "There's nothing fancy about this situation."

"Honey, you're pregnant by a man you despise. You have to admit it is sort of funny. When are you going to tell him?"

"Never," Emily answered as she nursed a glass of milk in her father's kitchen.

"But you have to tell him. He's the father."

Emily corrected him. "He's a sperm donor."

"Bekim would make a wonderful father, and just think of all the beautiful maternity clothes he could design for you."

"And think of the many women your grandchild would be calling Auntie. Bekim doesn't have time to be a father. He has an active social life."

Solomon poured himself a glass of milk and joined her at the table. "Not lately. He's in a slump."

"He is a slump," Emily said. *A very sexy slump.*

"How is Megan Jefferies' collection coming along?" Solomon asked.

She, Shane and Deandria had been pulling some pretty long hours lately. Tonight she agreed to meet Bekim over at his place to look over his design for some formal wear. She'd just stopped in to give her father the news away from the gossipers at work. Emily finished her milk, rose and put the glass in the sink.

"Don't work too late," Solomon told her. "You're going to need a lot of rest now that you're pregnant."

"I know," Emily said. "I'll leave Bekim's as soon as I check the designs." She kissed Solomon on the head and left the house.

* * * *

Bekim led Emily into the apartment and to his drawing room. "Have you eaten?" he asked.

"No," she said. "I plan to pick up something on the way home."

"You really need to eat," he said. "You're feeding another mouth now."

"I know this. I've been able to eat more now since the morning sickness stopped."

"And you need to think about wearing flatter heels. You could trip and fall."

Emily looked down at the drawings and smiled. Bekim was worried about her.

"Are you seeing a doctor?"

"Yes, I have an appointment next week."

"You should have the baby's father go with you."

"I'll think about it," Emily said. "Hey, I like this one. It's just perfect for someone with a petite build."

"Have you purchased any maternity wear yet?" Bekim asked.

"No. Why?"

"Let me design them for you."

Emily looked up from the drawing. "You have enough to do. Shane can whip me up something."

Bekim frowned at her. "I thought you didn't want anyone else to know. Is he the baby's father?"

Emily laughed. "Hell no. Shane's nice, but I have no interest in him."

"Then who is he?" Bekim moved closer to her.

"No one you know," Emily answered. "Can we get back to the drawings?"

"I'm serious. All I need to do is take a few quick measurements. I'll make you look like a queen."

Emily thought about it. What harm could it do? "Okay."

"I can't believe you're agreeing so easy," Bekim said.

"I only agreed so you will stop badgering me. Besides you might do me something nice and appropriate for my age."

Bekim walked away from her and pulled out a tape measure. "You need to undress."

"You mean you want to take my measurements now?"

Bekim nodded. "The sooner the better. You can change behind the shade." Wasn't it a screen last time?

Emily walked away from the drafting table and went behind the shade to disrobe. She didn't know why she bothered since he'd seen everything she had anyway. Moments later she stepped out in her underwear and bare feet.

She followed Bekim's gaze from her breasts to her belly.

"Damn, I had no idea you were this far along. When's the baby due?"

"April," Emily answered.

Bekim walked over with the tape measure and measured her shoulders first. "That would make you almost five months."

"Yes," she said as he measured her around the chest.

"You're going to need bigger bras too. You're spilling out your cups."

She would have considered the comment rude had it been some average Joe off the streets, but Bekim knew bras. "I have them on order."

Bekim lowered the tape measure to her belly. "You're going to need something with pleats and elastic to adjust to your bulge." He paused. "If the baby is due in April that would mean you got pregnant sometime in July."

"Something like that," Emily said. *Oh lord, he's going to figure it out.*

"That was around the time of the company picnic." He dropped the tape. "Shit." Bekim grabbed her by the shoulders. "Please tell me it isn't so."

Emily trembled in his grasp. "It isn't so."

"Then who?"

Emily gulped. "Someone. I don't remember."

His grip tightened. "Don't give me that, shit, Emily. Are you carrying my baby?"

Emily sighed. "Yes."

Bekim removed his hands. "Why didn't you tell me?"

"I have my reasons," she said.

Bekim reached down and picked up the tape.

Emily stepped back behind the shade to change.

"What possible reason could you have for not telling me?" His cell phone rang. "Hello? Oh hello Simone," he said.

Emily walked out from around the shade fully dressed. She reached for her purse. "You don't have time to be a father," she told him. "I can't compete with your women."

Chapter Five

The lovely clothes kept arriving after Emily thought she made it clear she didn't want anything to do with Bekim. By Thanksgiving she gave up trying to hide her belly and allowed her father to announce he was finally going to be a grandfather to anyone who would listen. Of course, everyone speculated on the identity of the father, and Emily just gave up on this too since Bekim walked around the company on a cloud and watching her with big puppy dog eyes. She also gave in and agreed to let Bekim accompany her on her next prenatal appointment. But before then she just had to get through Thanksgiving dinner with Bekim, Solomon and Bekim's family, whom she'd never met.

"How difficult can this be?" Solomon asked, as he and Emily rode in the backseat of his town car.

Emily gazed over at him. "It won't be difficult for you. You're not the one with the future little Bekim in the oven."

Solomon reached over and patted her hand. "I'll be with you every step of the way."

The Bekim family home was located in the Upper East Side of Manhattan. It was in fact a villa near Seventy-Third Street and astonishingly not too far from her grandfather's mansion.

"How long have you known Bekim's family lived near grandfather?" Emily asked.

"Quite a while," Solomon said. "His family is filthy rich, but a bit eccentric."

Talk about the kettle calling the skillet black. Emily looked ahead. The manor overlooked the East River. It was a huge two-story brick Colonial with a matching brick privacy fence. "Is this for real?" Emily asked as she continued to stare at the place. The driver drove them up a winding driveway.

"So, your baby's going to be a little pampered," Solomon said.

Pampered? The kid would be rotten to the core, just like his father.

The driver got out and helped Emily and Solomon from the car and then he removed some gifts from the trunk and followed the Bucktells up to the front door.

Solomon rang the doorbell and minutes later a butler answered. Solomon introduced himself.

"Right this way, Sir." The butler led them down a marbled hallway into a huge waiting area and then down another hall to the formal dining room.

Emily kept eyeing the priceless art, the gorgeous Persian rugs and the adorable little dark-haired girl who followed the butler.

The butler opened a door and stepped inside the dining room. He took the gifts from the driver and placed them on a table. Then he announced Emily and Solomon and left with the driver. The little girl giggled and ran over to a young woman who also had dark hair. There was another little dark-haired girl present.

Bekim stood up and walked toward them. He looked like someone from the Roaring Twenties with his hair slicked back and wearing a formal dressed suit. Emily did like the color. It was a medium gray with a dark gray vest.

"Emily, Solomon," he said rather formerly. "I'm glad you're here. Please let me introduce you to my family."

They followed him up to the table.

"Mother and father, this is Solomon Bucktell and his daughter Emily. Emily and Solomon, these are my parents Martin and Isadora Lacolmn."

The Lacolmns rose.

Martin reminded Emily a lot of her own father, except Martin had brown hair and probably didn't cheat on his wife. He wasn't quite as tall as Bekim or Solomon, but he still had a great build and Bekim's blue eyes.

Isadora was a smartly dressed woman with short stylish black hair and a pretty smile. She shook Solomon's hand, but hugged Emily. "Welcome to our family, dear," she said. Once she released Emily she just stood there staring at her for a few minutes, especially around the midsection. "That outfit is simply gorgeous. Did Bekim design it for you?"

"Yes, Mrs. Lacolmn," Emily said.

"Call me, Dora, dear. And you have dark hair too. I wonder if the baby will have your green eyes or be blue like Bekim's."

When did we get on this subject?

"Come. Let me introduce you to the others." Dora led her away from her father and the other men. "This is Glenda and her husband Tad."

The young woman did resemble Bekim around the eyes.

"It's nice to meet both of you," Emily said "And this is?" she asked of the little girl on Glenda's lap.

"This is Caroline. Say hello to Miss Emily, Caroline."

Caroline had big blue eyes and appeared to be about three years old.

"Hello," she said shyly.

Dora took Emily around to the next couple. Both husband and wife had black hair. "This is Charity and Clark," she said.

Charity rose to greet Emily. "I thought Bekim exaggerated, but no. You are so beautiful."

Valley girl?

"You'll have to excuse my wife," Clark said with a smile. "She doesn't get out much."

Charity leaned over and playfully punched Clark on the arm. "I do so."

"Are you Uncle Bekim's girlfriend?" the other little dark-haired girl asked Emily.

"Yes, sweetie," Charity answered. "This is Empress," she told Emily. "Uncle Bekim and Aunty Emily are going to have a baby."

The bomb went off in Emily's head. She'd gone from Miss Emily to Aunty Emily in less than ten minutes, and she didn't even know these people.

"I'm glad you're his new girlfriend," Empress said. "I didn't like the other one."

Emily smiled at the child. She didn't like any of Bekim's girlfriends either.

Bekim stopped talking with the men and walked over to them. "I see you've met the precocious one," he said of Empress.

"She's adorable," Emily said.

"Can I play with the baby?" Empress asked her uncle.

"Sure sweetie, in about four months. But right now I think it's time to sit down and eat."

Bekim took Emily's hand and led her to the other side of the table. Dora followed them.

* * * *

It didn't take Emily long to understand what Solomon meant about the Lacolmns. They were a fun and loving family discussing every topic under the sun while they went through course after course of delicious food. After dinner the men went to the library for cigars and wine, while the women went to the parlor to have tea.

Emily would have preferred to drink tea with the women, but Bekim insisted she go with him to take a tour of his home.

"Your family is…"

"Strange," Bekim finished for her.

"I wasn't going to say that," Emily said with a smile. "I was going to say nice. I thought they'd treat me like a pariah."

Bekim walked her around the outside of the manor. The place had a lovely view of the East River.

"Now why would you think that? You're the first pregnant woman I've brought home."

Emily rolled her eyes at him. "But you have brought other women home to meet them."

Bekim sighed. "I'm not an angel, Emily. They've met every woman I've dated, but so far you're the only one they like."

"You mean they didn't like Camille? I wonder why."

Bekim smiled. "No, they didn't. Camille takes some getting used to."

"She's an airhead," Emily said. "Do you miss her?"

"Yes," Bekim admitted. "But I hope she's happy with her new man."

"Would you be less happy for her if I wasn't pregnant?" Emily asked.

"No," Bekim said as they strolled by a huge swimming pool. "Camille and I had a good run, but it's time to grow up."

"You don't have to grow up just for me, or give up your other girlfriends. I can manage just fine on my own."

Bekim took her hand and pulled her toward him. "Don't do this to me Emily. I want to be a part of our child's life. I want to be a part of your life and be there every step of the way."

Emily pulled away. "You say this now, but what will you do when the next beautiful model or starlet comes your way?"

"I'll be too busy changing diapers to care. I know you don't believe me, but I'm serious. I can't wait to accompany you to your next prenatal visit. I have a lot to learn and I plan to ask the doctor a lot of questions."

She wished she could believe him. "Your nieces are so cute." Emily said as they re-entered the manor.

"Yes, they are," Bekim said as he led her through a side door and up two flights of stairs.

"What's up here?" Emily asked.

"My bedroom," Bekim answered. "Or it was when I lived here."

Emily peeked into several other large rooms as they walked. Two of the rooms had dolls on the shelves and there was a quaint pink decorated bathroom situated between those two rooms.

Bekim stopped before a door and opened it. He took Emily's hand and tugged her inside and locked the door. He turned on the light. "This used to be my sanctuary," he said.

Emily never expected to see such a charming room. Besides a bed and some other furniture, Bekim had a great view of the gardens down below and some of the other homes in the neighborhood. The room had its own private bath and a small sitting area. She expected to see trucks and baseballs instead of an easel and a life-sized mannequin.

Emily walked over to the easel and flipped through some of the paper. "You drew these?" Emily asked as she admired some of his earlier dress designs.

"Yes, I always knew I'd design clothes, even as a child. I believed my parents thought I was going to be gay since I played with paper dolls and would make clothes for my sisters' dolls. I even drew bridal gowns."

Emily chuckled. "No, you're definitely not gay." She flipped another page. It was a bridal gown." I thought you were joking."

"Nope," Bekim said.

"How old were you when you drew this?"

"Sixteen," Bekim said.

Emily noted the intricate details and the talent of the young Bekim. "Has this particular gown been made yet?" She turned and found Bekim standing close behind her.

"No," he said. "You're the first person to ever see this drawing."

"But it's so beautiful. Why haven't you made it?"

"I'm just waiting for the perfect bride-to-be to come along," he said walking closer.

Emily gulped. The scent of his cologne made her giddy. "I'm sure she'll come along one day."

"You look very beautiful in this suit," Bekim said backing her up toward the bed.

"What are you doing?"

"I'm about to live out a fantasy."

"What?" Emily asked as he lifted her and carried her over to his bed.

"I've always dreamed of making love to a beautiful woman in this room while the family is downstairs unaware of what's going on upstairs."

"Bekim we can't," Emily protested.

"Why not?" Bekim asked as he kissed her on the cheek.

"They might hear us."

"So," Bekim said. "They already know we have a sexual relationship," he said touching her stomach.

He had her out her clothes before she could protest again. Bekim entered her slowly at first, but soon the two of them were swept away by passion. They came almost simultaneously.

"I wanted to do this from the moment you walked into the dining room," Bekim said. He kissed her gently on the lips. "I must be the only man in the world who gets turned on by the color yellow."

It was hard for Emily to think with Bekim still all up in her stuff and growing hard again as he planted kisses to her face. "You designed the suit to flatter my figure," Emily said with a gasp as Bekim spread her legs apart with his and went back to humping her passionately. She had to bite her bottom lip to keep from screaming as he took her over the edge again. Bekim came again emptying his seed inside her.

"I can make love to you all afternoon," Bekim said as he rolled off her. "But I'm afraid the folks might come looking for us."

They climbed off the bed and entered the bathroom together for a quick shower. An hour later they rejoined the family downstairs. The men had joined the ladies in the parlor.

Charity just looked at her and smiled like she knew what had occurred upstairs between her and Bekim. She and Solomon left the Lacolmns about an hour later.

"I think Bekim's family likes you," Solomon told her on the way back to Emily's apartment.

"How can you tell?" Emily asked.

"They've begun taking bets on the baby's sex and on the date you and Bekim will marry."

"Huh?" Emily asked.

Solomon nodded. "Dora already has a room picked out for a nursery for when the baby visits, and Martin is planning to purchase some stock and bonds for the baby."

Everything was happening too fast. She and Bekim weren't dating and they certainly hadn't discussed marriage.

Solomon chuckled. "You look very afraid of the future."

"What future?" Emily asked. "I have to get past going to the obstetrician with Bekim on Monday."

Solomon reached over and patted her hand. "He'll be okay. Bekim is made of strong stock."

Emily snatched her hand away. "I'm not worried about him. I'm worried about me."

Chapter Six

Bright and early Monday morning Bekim appeared at Emily's door ready to accompany her to the prenatal visit. He brought her a big teddy bear to commemorate the event.

Emily put the teddy bear on the sofa, grabbed her purse and followed Bekim out the door. A chauffeured-driven car waited at the curb. "We could have taken the bus," Emily told him as he helped her into the back seat of the car.

"I know, but you could get jostled or you might fall exiting the bus." Bekim climbed in next to her and the chauffeur drove away from the curb and entered the traffic.

"Now you're just being silly. I can trip in the apartment."

"I've been meaning to talk to you about that," Bekim said. "Maybe you should move in with me until after the baby is born."

"Why?" Emily asked. Things were moving entirely too fast between them.

"Because you need someone to hold your hair when you vomit, and someone to make sure you eat and rest."

"I'm perfectly capable of doing this for myself, in my own apartment," Emily said. "If I get desperate enough I can move back in with my father."

Bekim laughed. "You wouldn't want to move back home with Solomon. You'd be under the control of one of his current girlfriends."

Emily grimaced. "I hadn't thought about that, but like I said before I'm perfectly capable of looking out for myself."

"For now," Bekim said. "But in two months you won't be able to tie your shoes. Hell, you won't be able to see your feet."

"You always have to have the last word don't you?" Emily asked.

"Yes. What did you eat for breakfast this morning?"

"Nothing yet," Emily said.

"See, the baby needs nourishment even if you don't feel like eating. I'll fix you breakfast after we return from the doctor's office."

"What about work?" Emily asked.

"What about it? It will still be there tomorrow."

"I didn't plan to take the entire day off. My father will be worried."

"No he won't," Bekim told her. "I've already spoken to him this morning. He said have fun."

Emily grimaced. Was no one on her side? "I promised Deandria I would help her today."

"Deandria said she'd see you tomorrow and go right to bed after the doctor's visit."

Emily frowned. Even her best friend had turned against her. "I'll agree to take the day off, but the moving in with you will take some serious thinking over on my part."

"Okay," Bekim said. "I'll agree to just the breakfast for now." He settled back in the seat next to her.

Why did she feel like she'd lost the war?

The driver maneuvered his way through traffic until they finally arrived outside the Women's Clinic. Bekim helped her out the car "I'll call you when we're ready to leave," he told the driver. He and Emily walked toward the door and the driver drove away from the curb.

The obstetrician's office was on the fifth floor. Emily and Bekim rode the elevator up and then Emily led the way to the office. Bekim opened the door for her and they stepped inside. The office was already occupied with expectant mothers and fathers. Emily signed in, gave her insurance and identification cards to the receptionist and paid her co-pay. She and Bekim found seats next to a huge aquarium of salt-water fish and waited for Emily's name to be called.

A half-hour later Emily and Bekim walked to the back where Emily was weighed and told to change into a paper gown. Bekim joined her in the examining room and he talked to her while they waited for Doctor Kim to arrive.

Moments later the door opened and the doctor entered.

Emily introduced Bekim.

Doctor Kim took Emily's pressure and tested her pulse while Bekim sat in a chair listening closely to everything the doctor said.

Doctor Kim made Emily lay down on the table while he measured her stomach.

Bekim was on his feet now checking everything out personally. It didn't help matters much that her breasts and all her other goodies were exposed during the examination.

"I am going to listen for the baby's heartbeat now," Doctor Kim told them. He rubbed a cold gel all over Emily's stomach and moved a cold piece of equipment over it. "Found it," he said. Doctor Kim turned up a couple of controls on a monitor so they could hear.

Emily smiled when she heard the heartbeat.

"The baby has a strong heart," Doctor Kim said. "Would you care to see the baby?" He helped Emily to sit up.

Bekim looked down at the monitor and chuckled. "It's a baby," he announced.

"Most certainly," Doctor Kim said. "We should be able to determine the sex soon."

"We don't want to know," both Emily and Bekim said simultaneously.

"We're old fashioned," Bekim explained. "We want to be surprised."

Emily nodded in agreement.

Doctor Kim moved the monitor away and a nurse entered to clean the gel from Emily's stomach. "You can get dressed now and the two of you can meet me in my office," Doctor Kim said. He left and the nurse followed him out.

Bekim helped Emily down from the examination table and waited patiently while she dressed. They walked down the hall to Doctor Kim's office for their consultation.

"Please be seated," Doctor Kim said. "It's nice to speak with both parents. Mostly it's just the mother. The fathers miss out on so much by not coming along to some of the prenatal visits."

"I plan to be here with Emily every step of the way," Bekim said.

"Good," Doctor Kim said. "Emily's going to need someone there for her as the pregnancy advances. But don't get alarmed if her hormones go all wonky and she calls you names and tells you that she hates you."

"She already calls me names," Bekim said with a smile. "I can handle it."

Doctor Kim chuckled. "Good. You're going to need that sense of humor. Now let's see. Emily's weight and pressure are good. Her recent blood tests show no deficiencies. Hopefully she's taking the prenatal vitamins and Folic Acid I prescribed for her."

Why did she feel like she wasn't in the room?

"I want you to drink plenty of milk and eat nutritious foods like fruits and vegetables. You can also do some walking and a little exercise, but no heavy lifting or standing on your feet for long periods of time."

"How long can she continue to work?" Bekim asked.

"Most women work well into their eight month," Doctor Kim said. "But it all depends on Emily and the baby. If it gets to be too much I will recommend bed rest."

"I'll make sure she listens even if I have to get her father to help me."

"There will be no need for that," Emily said. "I will be good and do what I'm supposed to do."

"Good, then I'll see the two of you next month," Doctor Kim said. He opened a desk drawer and pulled out a book and a DVD disk and handed it to Bekim. "I recommend you read the book and view the video. It's Emily's body but you will be of more help to her if you know exactly what she's going through."

"Thank you," Bekim said rising. "I'll watch the video later."

Doctor Kim rose and then Bekim helped Emily to her feet. They left the office and Bekim called the driver back.

"Take us to my condo," he instructed the driver once they were back inside the car.

The driver went off again once they reached Bekim's place.

"There are some clothes for you in the other bedroom if you want to change into something more comfortable while I fix breakfast," Bekim told her. "And some slippers too. Your ankles look a bit swollen."

"Yes, Doctor Lacolmn," Emily said walking from the living room to the hall.

Bekim followed. "I need to change too." He disappeared into the master bedroom and Emily entered the guest room. All of Bekim's designs, his sewing machine and the bolts of material had been removed. In their place was a lovely new white bedroom suite, a rocking chair and a desk.

A maternity smock lay on the bed and a pair of soft slippers sat on the floor beside the bed. Emily took a few minutes to grasp the severity of what he'd done for her. Maybe she'd underestimated his sincerity.

Emily used the toilet and changed her clothes. It did feel good to get out the bra and heels and to slip into something less constricting. She sat down in the rocker to try it out. *I could get used to this*. Emily rose and tested the bed. *Good mattress*. She yawned, suddenly feeling tired. She didn't think Bekim would mind if she took a little nap before breakfast.

* * * *

Bekim looked down on Emily as she slept in the white bed. He'd come up to check on her when she didn't join him in the kitchen while he prepared breakfast. *You are so beautiful, Emily Bucktell. Motherhood certainly agrees with you.*

Emily moved on the bed when he sat down next to her. She opened her eyes. "How long have I been asleep?"

"Not long," Bekim said. "Breakfast is ready." He moved so Emily could get off the bed.

"I have to pee," she announced.

"That is to be expected," Bekim said. "Come down once you've finished." He left her and went back downstairs to the kitchen. Emily joined him several minutes later looking refreshed.

"I must have been asleep for a long time," Emily said as she sat down.

He'd prepared eggs, oatmeal, fresh squeezed orange juice, and wheat toast and turkey bacon. He fixed a cup of coffee for himself and put a glass of milk in front of Emily. After eating everything on her plate, Bekim placed a bowl of fresh fruit in front of Emily. She ate this too.

"I'm so full," Emily said pushing away from the table. "I couldn't eat another bite."

Bekim cleared the table and then he and Emily walked to the entertainment room to watch the video Doctor Kim gave him. Things were going along swimmingly until they got to the part with the baby being born. Emily turned an unhealthy shade of green. She hopped out her seat and ran to the bathroom. Bekim chuckled. He couldn't wait to be in the delivery room to find out if Emily would faint.

Chapter Seven

November disappeared as quickly as it arrived and soon Manhattan showed signs of Christmas.

Bekim started attending prenatal classes with Emily. He was doing his best to be good, but Emily passed out every time the instructor showed a birthing film.

Several of the expectant mothers and the teachers flirted openly with Bekim. Bekim, being Bekim naturally flirted back.

Emily and Bekim flew off to France for a conference and returned just before Christmas. The trip was fun and he was very attentive to her needs. She introduced him to some of her friends and colleagues and most of them congratulated them on the upcoming birth of their baby.

He finally talked her into moving in with him. Solomon was thrilled at the idea of his daughter shacking up with his best designer. The rest of the employees had a bet on how long the two of them would live together without killing each other.

Emily's hormones kicked in sooner than she expected. One minute she'd be fine and before she knew it she'd be crying over the smallest thing. Both Bekim and Shane worked their asses off to meet Solomon's Christmas deadline, and both of them had to suffer through Emily's period of ranting and raving when things didn't go exactly on schedule.

"You have the two of them terrified," Deandria told her as the two of them snuck off for lunch and for a little girl time. Bekim's two sisters Charity and Glenda who'd come to town to shop for Christmas joined them.

"I don't mean to scream at them," Emily as she ate her chef's salad.

"It's the hormones," Charity assured her. "I was the same way with

Clark when I was pregnant with Caroline."

"Me too," Glenda said. "Tad would spend most of his days at work and then cowering in the den at night just so he didn't have to deal with me."

"Bekim doesn't hide from me," Emily said. "He's always very attentive and very helpful. I don't think I've ever seen him angry before."

"Emily is right," Deandria said. "Bekim escorts her around like a boy scout and makes sure she eats her vegetables."

"Bekim has always been kind and considerate," Glenda said. "Even as a child. It was like having a third sister."

All four women laughed.

"Sex is so much better when you're pregnant," Charity said.

Glenda agreed with her. "You don't have the fear of getting pregnant so you're more relaxed."

All three women looked at Emily.

"How is Bekim in the sack?" Glenda asked her.

Emily nearly choked on her salad. "I don't think I should be discussing this with his sisters."

"You can tell me," Deandria said. "I'm your best friend."

She didn't think she should tell intimate details to Deandria either. "He's very good. I have no complaints."

Deandria chuckled. "You're just being modest in front of his sisters."

"Okay, he's fantastic in bed."

Glenda and Charity laughed.

"Mother thinks you're the perfect match for Bekim," Glenda said once she stopped laughing. "I've never seen her so excited."

"I like Dora too," Emily said. "I can't wait to talk with her again at the Christmas party."

This year Bucktell was hosting a big party for the employees and their families. Solomon rented a hall and a band and arranged for the catering.

Shane already designed a maternity outfit for her after getting Bekim's permission. And it was to be her and Bekim's first official date as a couple.

"I have to pee," Emily announced. She stood up. "I'll be back shortly." The three other women went on talking like she wasn't even

63

there. They were still deep in conversation when she returned.

The four women finished their lunch. Glenda and Charity went off to shop while Emily and Deandria walked back to the fashion house.

Solomon was supervising the decorating of the display room windows when they returned.

Shane and Bekim were doing the bulk of the work under Solomon's supervision. Bekim waved to them as he dressed a mannequin.

Bekim took her out to dinner after work and later that evening they watched a movie together. Bekim had chosen a love story, which brought Emily to tears by the end.

"Stupid hormones," she said as she wiped the tears away.

"Sleep with me in my room tonight," Bekim said to her before the movie ended.

"Why?" Emily asked. She was quite comfortable sleeping in the white bedroom.

Bekim took her hand and placed it on his lap. His cock moved beneath her palm. "This is why."

"Oh," Emily said. They hadn't made love since the time at Bekim's parents' home.

"I've been thinking about you all day," he said. "Did you have a lovely time with my sisters?"

"Yes," Emily said absently massaging his dick. "They are very fond of you."

"That's because I design clothes for them. Ooh, squeeze it."

Emily squeezed Bekim's cock.

Bekim moaned and stopped the video. "We can watch the rest of this later." He rose, took her hand and led her upstairs to his bedroom.

* * * *

The next morning Emily woke up buck-naked with Bekim cuddled up next to her. She didn't remember how many times he made her come during their night of lovemaking, but her body felt loose as well as sticky from his semen.

The alarm sounded and Bekim opened his eyes. "Good morning, sweet Emily. Let's shoot hooky from work today."

"We can't stud," Emily said trying to move out his arms. "The big Christmas party is tonight and I promised I'd help my father with some last minute things."

"Shoot" Bekim said, pretending to be disappointed. "I wanted to feed my son again."

Emily chuckled sarcastically. "The baby could very well be a girl."

"It's a boy," Bekim said releasing her and crawling out the bed. "I have two sisters and two nieces. I have to be the one in my family carrying the boy gene."

Emily laughed. "What if the baby's a girl?"

"Then she'll be the first girl on the block with a football and a catcher's mitt."

Emily crawled off the bed. "Ooh. I'm all sticky."

"It's great for the skin," Bekim assured her as he walked across the room naked.

Emily's nipples hardened at the sight. "I supposed we could be a couple of minutes late."

"Huh?" Bekim asked stopping in his tracks. "Oh," he said. "Your nipples are huge." He hurried back to bed and hopped in.

Emily joined him. "And whose fault is that?" she asked as she opened her legs and invited Bekim in.

"Definitely mine," Bekim said as he thrust deeply inside her. "Ooh, you feel so good. We are so going to be late for work."

* * * *

The last person Emily expected to see at the Christmas party was Camille. She arrived alone.

"What's she doing here?" Deandria asked.

Emily shrugged. She hadn't seen Camille in three months and the woman's presence hadn't been missed.

"I wonder if she's still with that guy." Deandria asked.

"Who cares?" Emily asked as she sipped her punch.

"You should care," Deandria said. "If she's broken up with him then she might want to get back with Bekim."

Emily shook her head. Bekim wouldn't get back with Camille, would he?

Bekim was on the dance floor kicking up his heels with his mother. Solomon was dancing with his current girlfriend Eva, a socialite who appeared to be about two years older than Emily. The rest the Lacolmns were also on the dance floor. Deandria's date was in the restroom.

"I don't own Bekim," Emily said.

Camille wore a stunning blue gown that molded to her statuesque body. Several men flocked toward her as she sauntered into the room.

"If I was her I wouldn't show my face after what she did to Bekim."

"Me either, Shane said coming up between them. "But some women have no class."

Shane's date went off the ladies room and left him there for her and Deandria to watch over him.

The music ended and everyone headed back to their seats. Bekim was on his way back over to her when he spotted Camille.

"What do you supposed they're discussing?" Shane asked.

Emily shrugged. *Yes, what indeed?* Her father and Eva walked over to join them.

Both Shane and Deandria's dates returned and pulled them on the dance floor leaving her alone to nurse her glass of punch.

Martin Lacolmn approached and asked Emily to dance.

"I might as well since Bekim is busy," Emily said.

"My son isn't a fool," Martin said as he slow danced Emily around the dance floor. "I understand Camille left him for another man."

"You know about that?" Emily asked. Martin was a real good dancer.

"Yes. Bekim told me about her and about you."

"I'm surprised he mentioned me in the same breath as Camille."

"No, he mentioned your name years before he met her," Martin said. "I believe it was right after he went to work for your father. I think he called you a spoiled rotten princess." Martin chuckled. "And then he called you a Dragon Queen."

"Yeah, well I've called him quite a few names too since we've met," Emily said.

"He will make a good father," Martin said. "I remember how good he was with Caroline and Empress when they were babies. Bekim used to walk the floor with them at night when they were colicky and he even gave them baths and dressed them."

"He's expecting a boy," Emily explained to Martin. "He wants to play ball now instead of dressing dolls."

"Well, it would be nice, but he'll just have to be happy with a girl if one arrives."

The music ended and the two of them headed back to the table where the rest of the family was seated. Bekim walked Camille over to the table later.

"It is nice to see you all again," Camille said to the Lacolmns.

"Aren't you going to speak to Emily?" Bekim asked Camille.

"But of course Be-kim. How are you Emily?"

Emily rose and Camille's eyes dropped to Emily's stomach. "I'm fine Camille."

Camille pointed. "You're preggers."

"She sure is," Bekim said, leaving Camille's side and putting his arms around Emily's waist. "Our baby is due in about three and a half months."

His statement left Camille almost speechless. "Your baby Be-kim? I thought she hated you."

"Apparently not," Bekim said, kissing Emily on the cheek. "Doesn't she look wonderful?"

"Yes, she does," Camille said. "Well, Merry Christmas to all of you. I just stopped by to see everyone. I'm headed to another party in the neighborhood." She turned on her heels and beat a hasty retreat out the hall.

"Don't use me for revenge," Emily told Bekim, punching him in the gut playfully.

"Okay sweetheart," Bekim said helping her into a seat and sitting down next to her. "Ouch, you're strong."

Martin chuckled. "Serves you right son," he told Bekim. "Emily's no dummy."

Chapter Eight

By January everyone was once again getting ready for Fashion Week. Bekim had already put in some pretty long hours and would come home late at night after she'd gone to bed. Emily would help out as much as she could at the fashion house, but both Bekim and Solomon insisted she take a nap after lunch and then leave exactly at five so she wouldn't tire herself out.

Everything was finished by February and just in time for the big fashion shows.

Camille showed up late on the first day of the event and got into an argument with some of the models whom Emily had been working with for months. Of course, she didn't speak to Emily, which didn't faze her a bit. Camille donned the outfits Bekim designed for her and strutted her stuff on the catwalk like she owned it. She even threw her arms around Bekim and tried to kiss him on the last day of the fashion show. They were backstage and hadn't noticed Emily.

"Down girl," Emily overheard Bekim tell the model. "I'm spoken for, remember?"

"Emily doesn't have to know," Camille said.

"Yes, she does," Bekim told her. "We are in a relationship."

"But she's so old," Camille said. "And she doesn't have a sense of humor."

"I love her," Bekim said. "Now run along like a good girl and find yourself a new play toy."

Camille pouted and stalked off to the dressing room.

Afterward Bekim invited everyone out to dinner once they put away the clothing and shipped them back to the fashion house. Emily declined

68

because she was tired.

"It won't be the same without you," Bekim told her.

"I'll be okay," Emily said. "I need to rest."

Bekim rubbed her stomach. "Make sure you eat something nutritious. I won't be late."

"Okay," Emily said as he walked her out to the sidewalk and hailed her a taxi. He kissed her goodbye and cab peeled away from the curb.

Emily's dinner consisted of a pint of Cookie Dough Ice Cream and about four double chocolate brownies. She woke up and found Bekim looking down at her.

"Please tell me you didn't eat the entire pint of ice cream?"

"Okay, then I won't tell you," Emily said sitting up.

Bekim sat down beside her and licked dried ice cream and brownie crumbs from her face. "You know you shouldn't be eating junk food."

"It was a craving," Emily told him. "How was dinner?"

"Everyone had a good time," Bekim said loosening his tie. "What time does your plane leave tomorrow?"

"Eight," Emily answered. She was going on a short business trip to California and would be returning in a few days.

"You will be back in time for Valentine's Day won't you?"

"Yes," Emily said. "Did Camille join you guys for dinner?"

"When have you ever known Camille to miss out on a free meal?" Bekim asked.

"Oh, oh," Emily said. She sprang to her feet and grabbed her stomach.

"What's wrong?" Bekim asked.

"The baby doesn't like Cookie Dough Ice Cream." She ran to the bathroom before she threw up all over the entertainment room.

* * * *

"What time is Emily's plane coming in?" Bekim asked Solomon.

"Four," Solomon answered. "I'm sending the driver for her."

"Do you think she'll be here by seven?"

Solomon put down the newspaper he was reading and watched Bekim pace the floor. "What's going on at seven?"

"I've made dinner reservations for us," Bekim said. "And this." He pulled a small box from his pocket and handed it to Solomon.

Solomon opened the box. "Very nice. This is for Emily isn't it?"

Bekim nodded. "Yes. Do you think she'll like it?"

"That's depends on what it's for," Solomon said.

Bekim rolled his eyes at his boss. "It's Valentine's Day and she's seven months pregnant with my baby. And I love her to death."

"Oh, I see," Solomon said. "It's a bribe and you plan to make an honest woman out of her."

Bekim nodded again. "It's the least I can so. Did I mention that I love her?"

"Several times," Solomon said handing him back the box. "You know you can't spring something like this on Emily. You have to ease your way in there."

"I have reservations at an expensive restaurant and I have a beautiful red dress waiting for her at home."

"Sounds like a solid plan to me," Solomon said.

"Do you think I have any chance in getting her to accept?"

"I'd say you have a fifty-fifty chance of her turning you down," Solomon answered.

Bekim put the box back into his pocket. "That was cruel."

Solomon laughed. "You knew what you were getting into the moment you fell in love with her."

* * * *

Emily's plane arrived on time and Bekim made Solomon promise to have Emily dropped off at his place by six.

Emily arrived at five-thirty looking tired, but beautiful. He helped her in with her things and had a nice warm bath waiting for her. Bekim surprised her with the dress.

"It's beautiful," Emily said with a yawn. "What's it for?"

"For a dinner date," Bekim said. "We have reservations for seven."

Emily glared at him. "Okay, since you're already gone to all the trouble."

"We have to get ready quickly," Bekim said, dashing out the white room and into his own room. He donned a new black suit and met Emily in the hall thirty minutes later. He whisked her out of the condo and into the car.

Emily spoke to the chauffeur, yawned and laid her head against the back seat for a short nap.

Bekim woke her when they arrived at the restaurant. They made it there with five minutes to spare.

The restaurant was filled with other diners out celebrating

70

Valentine's Day. The waiter brought dessert after a scrumptious meal and music from a violinist. It was angel food cake topped with whipped crème and fresh berries.

"I have something for you," Bekim said to Emily after she devoured the cake and after she'd returned from the ladies room.

Emily sat down in her seat and Bekim walked over to her and knelt down on one knee.

"What's wrong with you?" Emily asked staring down at him and using her very annoyed Dragon Queen voice.

Bekim pulled the small box from his pocket and handed it to her.

"What's this?" Emily asked opening the box. She gasped. "It's a ring."

"Emily Bucktell, would you do me the honor of becoming my wife?" Bekim asked. He didn't think his heart could take it if Emily turned him down in front of a restaurant filled with people.

"Yes," Emily said meekly.

Bekim hopped to his feet. "She said, yes!"

The people around them clapped.

Bekim took the ring from Emily and slid it on her finger.

"It's beautiful," Emily said. "But can we go home now. I think I have jet lag."

Bekim paid the bill and whisked Emily out the restaurant and into the car. Thirty minutes later they were back at his place and Emily was sound asleep in the white room. *Sleep tight princess.*

Bekim crept out the room and walked downstairs. He picked up the telephone and dialed Solomon. "She said yes, Father."

Solomon chuckled. "Congratulations and welcome to the family. I'll talk to you tomorrow, but right now I'm on a date."

Bekim hung up the phone and went up to his room smiling from ear to ear.

Chapter Nine

"Surprise," a room full of women said as Emily entered the restaurant where she planned to have lunch with Deandria. But instead she found most of the women she knew, a chair decorated with baby things and a pile of presents stacked in a playpen.

Charity and Glenda led her to the seat of honor. Empress and Caroline were also there dressed in matching yellow dresses, yellow ankle socks and black patent leather shoes.

"Surprise, Aunty Emily," Empress said. "It's a baby party."

Emily hugged Empress. "Thank you, honey."

There were party games, lots of talk about babies and plenty of food. But before Emily could open the presents Dora had a surprise for her.

Deandria pressed a button on the wall near the light switch and a projection screen came down from the ceiling.

"It's a movie," Empress told her.

Dora pushed a button on the projector and the movie began. It was a film about a pregnant young woman standing in snow.

"It's me," Dora announced to them.

The scene changed and Dora was on a gurney at hospital and in labor. She could hear Martin in the background telling Dora that everything was going to be okay.

The next scene featured Dora holding a baby in her arms. The baby had dark hair so it was hard for Emily to tell which one of the Lacolmn siblings it was.

"It's Uncle Bekim," Empress informed her as a little dark-haired boy in a blue and white sailor suit ran through a field of grass.

"He was so cute." Emily said as scene after scene played on the screen of little Bekim.

The next scene showed a modern day Bekim. "Hello Emily dearest. If you're watching this film it means my mother and the other ladies have successfully tricked you into showing up at your baby shower they've been planning for months. But I have a surprise for you too. Two surprises to be exact." The camera panned in on a lovely brick Colonial home. Bekim walked up to the door. "Come on inside."

The cameraman followed him inside the charming brick home. Bekim began telling her the history of the home, taking them through five bedrooms, three baths, a huge kitchen and several other rooms. Finally Bekim opened a door and stepped inside a room. it was a nursery and furnished with all the furniture he and she picked out a couple of months ago. "It's our new home," Bekim announced. "A baby should be raised in a loving home and not in an apartment."

Emily gasped. "He didn't."

"He did," Glenda said. "It's our grandfather's home. Bekim had it remodeled just for you."

Tears of joy seeped from Emily's eyes. She'd always wanted a home like this. "The big lug."

The cameraman followed Bekim from the house to the House of Bucktell. The scene changed again. "Now for the second surprise," Bekim said. He opened the door to the small showroom. There were children mannequins on display with some cute clothing. "This is my new line of clothing," Bekim announced. "It's called the Baby B Collection." He held up an adorable white christening outfit. "This is for Bekim, Junior's Christening Day."

Emily laughed. "He's so sure it's a boy," she told everyone.

"Or this is for Emily, Junior's Christening Day," Bekim said holding up a white christening gown. "You see, Emily dear, I'm prepared for anything. The line launches tomorrow and will be featured in several fine department stores in the United States and France. Enjoy your shower Emily. I love you."

The film ended and the women clapped and congratulated her.

"I am going to strangle him," Emily told Dora once the shower ended. "What type of man does all of this without his fiancé knowing?"

"Bekim," Dora answered giving Emily a hug. "If you think this is something, wait until you see all the gifts that have been arriving from family and friends all around the country. At this rate you and Bekim will have to move in with us and use your new home as storage."

* * * *

"Where's Emily?" Solomon asked Bekim about a week later.

"She's home on bed rest," Bekim told his future father-in-law.

"And she's actually home in bed?"

"She was when I left home," Bekim said. "She can't get around as well as she thinks she can. She can only come out for doctor appointments or to take a little walk around the neighborhood for exercise. Other than that she is supposed to stay in bed with her feet elevated."

"Nice trick if you can pull it off," Solomon said.

"I promised her I'd take off Friday so we can sneak off to the Justice of the Peace."

"What? I thought the two of you would have a big wedding."

"Yes, we plan to do that after the baby is born. But Emily insists we be married before the baby arrives."

"I understand," Solomon said. "She's making sure you don't run out on her before you sign the birth certificate."

"No chance of that happening," Bekim said. "I'm going to be right there with her in the delivery room to cut the umbilical cord."

Solomon made a face. "I was pacing the waiting room floor with a lot of other expectant fathers when Emily was born. I didn't get to see her until she was cleaned up and in an incubator."

"I'll be right there in the delivery room acting as Emily birthing coach," Bekim told Solomon. "I'll be manning the camera and catching every moment of the delivery on film."

"You are a glutton for punishment, aren't you?"

Bekim nodded. "Emily will have to be on her best behavior because I plan to keep the tape to show the family."

Solomon laughed. "It's your funeral."

* * * *

Emily was going stir crazy after two weeks of bed rest and a quickie wedding at the Justice of the Peace. She was now Mrs. Bekim Lacolmn and she hadn't seen much of her husband lately except for in passing. Bekim's new baby line of clothing was a smashing success and orders were pouring in from everywhere.

Emily kept herself busy preparing dinner for Bekim when he came home and addressing Thank You cards for all the baby gifts they'd received. Bekim also hired a housekeeper to come in twice a week to clean and do the laundry.

Glenda and Charity paid her a visit on Monday and they kept her company for the rest of the day.

The phone in Bekim's home office rang just as Emily was coming back from fixing herself a sandwich and a glass of milk. The answering machine picked up the call before Emily could get to it.

"Hello, Bekim. This is Natalie. I'm flying into town tomorrow and I'm looking forward to meeting you on tomorrow night for dinner and dancing." She rattled off the name of her hotel and left a phone number.

The only Natalie she knew was an actress Bekim dated when he first came to work for her father. Emily continued on to the white room and fell asleep before Bekim came home from work.

The next evening Bekim called her and told her that he was working late. He returned home later drunk and reeking of perfume.

Emily feinted sleep and cried after Bekim stopped in the check on her. Bekim didn't understand why she was being so short with him the next morning. What the hell did he think she would do?

"Who is Natalie?" Emily asked Bekim as he got up to prepare Sunday breakfast for them.

"She's a friend," Bekim tried to explain.

"Did you go out with her last night?"

"Yes," Bekim answered.

"Why didn't you tell me? Why did tell me that you had to work late?"

"I thought you'd be upset," Bekim said.

"You thought right," Emily told him. She slapped his face and stormed back up the white bedroom. She continued to ignore Bekim for the rest of the month of March and into April.

Chapter Ten

"Where's the new husband?" Doctor Kim asked Emily as he examined her.

"Working," Emily answered, pretending not to feel discomfort with the doctor's fingers inside her. Doctor Kim removed his hand, changed gloves, and then measured her stomach. "It won't be long now. You're already dilating. How have you been feeling?"

"Tired," Emily said. "I feel like a beached whale and I'm fat from my face to my toes."

Doctor Kim chuckled. "That usually happens during pregnancy. You'll lose most of it right after delivery and you'll have to work the rest off with exercise."

"How's the baby?" Emily asked.

"The baby has a strong heartbeat and probably weighs close to nine pounds."

"I will be unconscious during the delivery won't I?"

Doctor Kim chuckled again. "No, you'll be just fine. Mister Lacolmn will be holding your hand throughout the entire event."

I'm not holding my breath.

Doctor Kim finished with the exam. "You can get dressed now. I want you to go straight home and get back into bed until the labor begins."

"I understand," Emily said. She didn't want anyone to see how big she'd gotten. She was even hiding from Bekim lately. Which didn't matter since he was working late every night and coming home long after she'd fallen asleep?

Emily left the clinic and got into the car. The driver drove away from the curb. Emily's cell phone rang. "Hello?"

"Hi honey, it's Daddy."

"Hey," Emily said.

"What are you doing?" Solomon asked.

"I'm just leaving the clinic. I had a doctor's appointment. Are you busy?"

"I'm always busy," Solomon told her.

"Can I drop by to see you?"

"You're supposed to be on bed rest."

"I'm near the fashion house," Emily said. "I won't stay long."

"Okay," Solomon said. "And then you have to go straight home. Bekim will kill me if I let anything happen to you."

Emily disconnected the call. "We're making a slight detour," she told the driver. "Take me to the House of Bucktell."

"Yes, Mrs. Lacolmn," the driver told her.

Moments later he helped her out the car and onto the sidewalk.

Emily entered the building and entered the elevator. The door closed and the elevator ascended up a couple of floors and then stopped. And not in a good way. The elevator was trapped between floors. Emily pressed a couple of buttons, but the elevator wouldn't budge. About an hour later her cell phone rang. "Hello?" Emily said.

"Where are you Emily, dear?" Solomon asked.

"I'm trapped in the damn elevator," Emily said. "It's stuck between floors."

"And you didn't think to call for help?" Solomon asked suddenly sounding concerned.

"Of course I did," Emily said. "The repairmen are on their way, but they're halfway across town. They told me to just sit and wait."

"How long ago was that?"

"About an hour," Emily told him. "And my water just broke."

"What?" Solomon asked loudly."

"My water just broke," Emily said.

"Why aren't you hysterical? Maybe I should call Bekim."

"Don't bother," Emily said. "He's probably too busy with Natalie or one of his other women."

"What are you talking about Emily?"

"Oh shit," Emily said as the first contraction it.

"What's wrong?" Solomon asked.

"I just had a contraction."

"I'm going to find Bekim," Solomon said. "Don't move." He disconnected the call.

"Funny guy," Emily said. "Where in the hell am I going?"

* * * *

"Emily baby are you okay?" Bekim asked when he finally called her.

"Sure," Emily said riding out another contraction.

"The elevator guys are stuck in traffic," Bekim told her.

"Great," Emily said. "I guess I'll just deliver the baby in the elevator."

"What?" Bekim asked. "Are you in labor?"

"Yes," Emily said. "Didn't my father tell you?"

"No. He just said you were trapped in an elevator."

"I love the man like a play step-cousin but he's no good in emergencies."

"Listen honey. I'm going to try to get you out."

"How? What are you going to do?"

"I'm going to try to climb down the elevator shaft."

"Are you insane? That's dangerous."

Bekim disconnected the call.

"He better not try something so stupid," Emily said aloud. Another contraction hit. "Ouch, ouch, ouch, shit." Emily heard a sound above her and then the elevator shook. *Oh Lord the elevator is going to fall.* She heard a loud noise again.

"Emily honey, are you okay?"

"Bekim are you crazy? The elevator might fall."

Bekim opened a little door on the roof of the elevator and slid in. "I was so scared," Bekim said. "I didn't want you to be alone. The elevator guys said they'll be here as soon as they can."

"My water broke," Emily said. "Watch how you step. You might slip."

Bekim maneuvered his way over to her just as another contraction hit. "Everything is going to be okay, baby. He took his jacket off and made a pillow for her.

Emily lay down with her head on his lap.

Bekim pulled out his cell phone and dialed the emergency number. "Hello, my name is Bekim Lacolmn. My wife and I are stuck in an elevator in the House of Bucktell Fashion Building," he told the dispatcher. He gave them the address. "The elevator repairmen are stuck in traffic and my wife is in labor."

"We'll have someone there as soon as possible," the dispatcher told him. "Don't panic."

Another hour passed. Sweat rolled down Emily's face and the contractions were coming more frequently.

"Why aren't you home in bed?" Bekim asked as he wiped her brow.

"I had a doctor's appointment and I thought I'd stop in to see my father."

"Oh, I forgot about the appointment," Bekim said. "Sorry, darling. I've been so busy."

"With Natalie," Emily said.

"No, of course not. Natalie just flew in town for one night. She and her husband wanted to go out to see New York."

"Her husband?" Emily asked. "She has a husband?"

"Yes," Bekim answered. "I told you Natalie and I are old friends. I introduced her to her husband and they were just in town for a short visit."

Emily felt so stupid. "I thought you were cheating on me. You came home that night drunk and reeking of perfume."

"I was drunk and I danced one dance with Natalie. She always wears too much perfume."

Another contraction hit. "Ouch," Emily moaned. "That hurt."

"Your contractions are about five minutes apart," Bekim told her. "If they don't fix the elevator soon we'll have some funny stories to tell our grandchildren."

"I am not having this baby in the elevator, Be-kim," Emily shouted as the pain hit her in the bottom of her stomach.

"You do a real good Camille," Bekim said.

"Not funny Be-kim," Emily said.

"Are you folks, okay in there?" someone shouted to them.

"Yes," both Emily and Bekim shouted back.

"We'll have you out of there in a couple of minutes."

"Hurry," Bekim said. "My wife is in labor."

The elevator repairmen got the door open five minutes later and an ambulance had been dispatched to take them directly to the hospital.

* * * *

Bekim got suited up in blue scrubs and entered the delivery room.

Emily's contractions were now a minute apart and Doctor Kim was with her trying to get her to push.

"Emily dear, I can see all the way up to your head," Bekim told her from the opposite end of the delivery table.

"Evil man," Emily said. "This is no time for jokes." She wasn't feeling any pain because the good anesthesiologist had given her an Epidural.

"I can see the baby's head," Doctor Kim announced. "Get ready to push."

Bekim got behind Emily and lifted her shoulder while the nurse pushed down on Emily's stomach.

"Push," Doctor Kim said.

Emily pushed and cursed Bekim in the same breath.

"You can relax now," Doctor Kim said chuckling. "Don't mind Emily. She is loopy from the medicine."

"It doesn't bother me a bit," Bekim said. "I'm capturing all this on tape." He'd set the camera up in the room and had it on automatic to free up his hands to help Emily.

"I'm going to need you to push again, Emily," Doctor Kim told her. "This time without the curse words. Push."

Emily pushed.

"You can relax," Doctor Kim said. "It's almost over."

Emily rested for a few minutes.

"Okay, we're going to do this one last time," Doctor Kim said. "This time I need a big push."

"I'm thirsty," Emily whined.

Bekim fed her some ice chips and then got back into position behind her back and lifted her again.

"Push," Doctor Kim said. "A big one."

Emily pushed.

"The head's out, and now the shoulders and now the rest of the baby," Doctor Kim said.

The next thing Bekim heard was a lusty cry.

"It's a boy," Doctor Kim said.

Bekim giggled like the Joker. "See I told you, Emily. I got me a son."

Doctor Kim chuckled. "Congratulations to both of you, Mister and

Mrs. Lacolmn. You'll get to see your son as soon as he's cleaned up and his vitals are taken."

"Thanks, Doctor," Bekim said. "And you too, Emily."

* * * *

Bekim looked down into the gray, possibly in the near future blue eyes of Bekim Alexander Lacolmn, Junior who entered the world weighing nine pounds and eight ounces. The boy also had a head of jet-black hair like his father.

Grandfathers Solomon and Martin passed out cigars to the men and the kisses to the womenfolk.

Emily lay unconscious in her hospital bed from some medication Doctor Kim gave her to relax.

"I don't see Emily in the baby," Solomon said. "Are you sure it's hers?"

"He has her attitude," Bekim said. "He's a fussy little guy."

"He looks just like Bekim did as a baby," Dora said. "But Baby B has more hair."

Bekim shook his head. The poor boy had a nickname already.

"You've spoiled him long enough," Dora told Bekim. "Let me hold my grandson."

Bekim rose from the chair, let his mother sit down and then handed her the baby.

"The baby is doomed," Charity said. "They are going to spoil him rotten."

"So will we," Glenda said. "I saw this precious sterling silver piggy bank in the mall. I think I'm going to drop over there later and get his name engraved on one."

Emily moved on the bed but didn't wake up.

"Your wife is missing out on all the fun stuff," Solomon told Bekim.

"She'll have all the fun she can stand once she takes the baby home," Bekim said.

Dora, Glenda and Charity laughed sarcastically.

"Yeah, she'll just love being woken up out of her sleep every night for feedings and diaper changes," Dora said to Bekim.

"I plan to help out," Bekim said.

"Sure," Martin said sarcastically. "I think I slept through your first year of life."

"You did, dear," Dora said. "Thank God for the nanny."

Bekim saw Emily open her eyes. "Hey, sleepy head."

"Hey," Emily said. "Did I have the baby yet?"

Bekim chuckled. "Yeah about four hours ago. Don't you remember?"

"No," Emily said. "I have a habit of blocking out things that hurt."

"Yes, I know," Bekim said thinking back to the first night they made love and the morning after.

Emily dozed off again.

Bekim bent down and kissed her on the head. "I'm going to miss this crazy doped up Emily."

"Yes, she'll be back to being the Dragon Queen just as soon as she returns to work," Solomon said.

"Urg," Bekim said. "Maybe I should keep her knocked up so she won't return to work."

"Don't even think about it," Emily said. "Two Bekims are enough in any family."

"I love you, honey," Bekim said as Emily dozed off again.

"Right back at you, designer boy." Emily said.

The End

About the Author

Imari Jade writes from Marrero, Louisiana, where she works full-time as a financial analyst. Her hobbies are reading manga and watching Asian movies. Imari short stories and novellas are features in several Mélange anthologies, and she's the author of the interracial, multicultural romance, "In Love with a Dark Stranger," released March 2011. Besides Mélange Books, Imari also writes for Sugar and Spice Press, Eternal Press, Siren-Bookstrand, Phaze Books, Total E-Bound, Passion in Print and just recently published her first Young Adult romance with Noble Books.

http://www.imarijade.com/
http://www.myspace.com/imarijade
http://imarijade.blogspot.com/

Other works by the author with Melange

In Love with a Dark Stranger
Skinship

Stories in Anthologies

Damnation in Forbidden Fruit Anthology
Love Never Dies in Halloween Hinjinx
Unwrapped Gifts in Holiday Treats
Wet in Love Afar
Bite Me in Midnight Thirsts
A Girl's Best Friend in Must Love Cats

Imari Jade ~ Daphne Olivier ~ Tori L. Ridgewood ~ Joanne Rawson

Rock-a-bye-Baby

by

Daphne Olivier

Imari Jade ~ Daphne Olivier ~ Tori L. Ridgewood ~ Joanne Rawson

Rock a-bye Baby
Daphne Olivier

"Cela! Hey, Cela, come take a look at this. My God, you're never going to believe this."

I heard Kane's call from the kitchen. I was busy selecting a menu for our evening meal, but the stunned disbelief in his voice made me switch off the auto-chef and head for the lounge.

"Believe what?" I asked, but instead of answering Kane gripped my arm and pointed to the Server-screen.

"Look—a Proc-permit! After all this time, a Proc-permit! Can you credit that?"

My jaw dropped. "Are you sure?"

"Of course I'm sure." Kane pressed the remote, the screen brightened and the letters doubled in size. "There, read it yourself."

I read it twice, and after the second scan allowed myself to believe that Kane was right. The document had 'Special Delivery Priority Mail' printed in bold letters across the top. The words below announced that Kane Barton Jackson, identity number 5682001497, and Cela Serena Jackson, identity number 9847107325, were the winners of the Draw, which took place on 21 July 2335. The recipients were advised that their selection entitled them to procreate and give birth to one live infant within a period of twelve months. Small print warned that if the couple failed to present themselves at the Procreation Centre within seven days, the privilege would be withdrawn.

I flopped onto the nearest couch. Kane sat down beside me. For a few seconds we just sat there, staring at the server-screen, and then he turned and asked, "So... what do you think?"

I blinked. "What do you mean? What's there to think about? It's what we've always hoped for, isn't it?"

He hesitated. "Well, yes, but that was when we were first married. Things have changed since then."

"In what way?"

"Well, let's face it, we're not as young as we used to be."

"We're not too old to have a baby," I pointed out. "Our names would have been removed from the Pool if that was so. The Law is very strict about that."

"I know. But, we've been married for over ten years."

I could feel my exasperation growing and found it difficult to keep my voice even. "What difference does that make?"

His voice took on an earnest tone. "A big difference. Look at it this way, Sweetheart. We're settled in our ways, got just about everything we ever wanted, good jobs, this house, the lakeside cottage, the shuttle, Betsy, Bonzo and Kitty. A baby, at this stage, would change everything."

Betsy, Bonzo and Kitty were the best models money could buy. Kane and I had paged through the catalogue and spent long hours calculating whether we could afford them, but in the end had decided to go for the best. We'd had no regrets. Betsy was not only smaller and lighter than old-fashioned domestics, but moved so quietly one hardly noticed she was there. Bonzo was a golden retriever, so well constructed it was almost impossible to tell he was not a real dog. Kitty, a blue-eyed Siamese, came from the same factory.

Kane put an arm around my shoulders, drawing me close. "I'll go with whatever you want, Sweetheart, but I want you to think things over carefully before you make up your mind."

I shook my head vehemently. "There's no need to think. I know what I want. I want..." That was as far as I got before he placed a finger on my lips.

"Hush. Hush. I want you to listen to what I have to say before you make a decision as important as this. Will you do that?"

I was disappointed to find Kane wasn't as enthusiastic as I was about the permit, but common sense told me it was only to be expected. Men were different from women. They lacked maternal instinct. And, besides, he was cautious by nature. He liked to turn things over a dozen times before reaching a decision. But he loved me, I knew he did, and it wouldn't do any harm to hear what he had to say. So I nodded and gave him a small smile. "Okay. Go ahead."

"I know you want a baby, Honey. I know it's been on your mind since the day we married, but I don't think you realize the implications, or just how much it would disrupt our lives. That's what we need to talk about."

"What do you mean?"

"Well, you'd have to give up your job for a start."

I tossed my head. "I know. I'm fully aware of that."

I liked my job at the library. I liked the people I worked with, I liked browsing through old books and manuscripts, and there was satisfaction in knowing that converting all that data to microchips and preserving it forever was a worthwhile job. It would be a wrench to give it up, but staying home to look after a baby would more than make up for it.

"Babies cry and need their nappies changed," Kane went on. "They need to be fed every few hours. They're messy little devils. And when they grow older they run around breaking things."

"I know. I know." And I really did know because although I'd never actually held a real, live baby in my arms, I'd read enough about them. That was what I enjoyed so much about my job. There was plenty of time to read, and a mountain of books to choose from, ancient books, written before the Catastrophe. And piles and piles of magazines. The ones I liked best had titles such as, 'Mother and Baby', 'The Toddler', 'Your Baby', and 'Baby Talk'. They contained articles about how to cope with temper tantrums, potty training, bedwetting, sibling rivalry and breastfeeding, to name but a few. I found a book written by a man called Dr. Spock most fascinating of all, and read it from cover to cover at least six times.

Kane's voice cut into my thoughts. "I'm making a suggestion. It's only a suggestion, Sweetie, so don't get in a state. But I'd like you to think about it for a few minutes."

"Think about what?"

"About adopting a RoBaby."

I sighed. We'd discussed the pros and cons of adopting a RoBaby more times than I could count. Most of our friends had accepted the fact there was little chance of them ever winning a Proc-Permit, and settled for adopting one, or even two, RoBabies. Kane had been keen to follow their example, but some instinct, deep inside of me, would not allow me agree. I did not want a baby made from Nu-plasma and wire and goodness knows what else. I'd grown attached to Bonzo and Kitty in the way one grows fond of a favourite toy, and Betsy was a real treasure, but the thought of nursing a RoBaby made me shudder.

I didn't feel like going over the old argument again, but knew that making a scene would get me nowhere, so I nodded and said, "Okay, I'm listening."

Kane smiled. "Good girl. I only want what's best for us, and there's a lot to be said for RoBabies."

"Such as?" I knew the answer, but asked anyway.

"They're cuddly and cute and smile and gurgle and coo, just like real babies. They cry too, but stop when they're told. They never get sick. They sleep through the night and don't whimper and whine if their mother forgets to feed them. Or change their nappy. RoBabies are smart, much smarter than real children. Most are programmed to talk right from day one. And there are thousands to choose from, all ages, all sizes, little redheads, blonds, brunettes, any colour and shape you fancy. If you get tired of the one you have, you can trade it in for a new model." Kane gave me an encouraging smile. "What do you say, Cela? Why not give it a try?"

I shook my head and jutted my jaw. "No, that's not what I want. I want a real baby, a baby that cries because it's hungry, or itchy, or tired, or just wants to be picked up and spoilt. A baby that needs me. Please, Kane, please."

He turned to search my face. "You're sure that's what you want"?"

"Quite, quite sure. Oh, Kane, it's what I want more than anything."

He hesitated a moment longer, then bent to kiss me. "Right. That's that then. I want you to be happy, Sweetheart. If you're absolutely sure this is what you want, I'll go along with it."

I threw my arms around his neck and kissed him right back.

* * * *

I could hardly contain my excitement when Kane and I climbed into the shuttle and set off for the Proc-Centre the following morning. From my window, I could see the city spread out below, a sprawl of houses, each surrounded by an expanse of green. Tree-lined streets crisscrossed the landscape, and here and there I glimpsed a lake set in a spacious park. No smog, no squalor, no slums. Not a high-rise building in sight. It was hard to believe that little more than a century ago, the city had teemed with tens of millions of people, jam-packed together like rats in an overcrowded cage.

It struck me that life might have gone on in the same way forever, if the X-virus had not appeared from nowhere, and decimated one city after another as it circled the globe. I was glad I'd been born in the new world, where such a catastrophe would never be allowed to happen again, but felt a little sad at the thought that so many pleasant things had disappeared with the bad. Like stork-parties and baby-showers and Father Christmas and stockings filled with toys. And nursery rhymes. One I'd come across in the library archive came back, and I began humming it under my breath, "Rock-a-bye baby on the tree top, when the wind blows the cradle will rock..."

We sped on, skimming trees and rooftops, then a flash of silver caught my eye and there was the Dome. The shuttle shot toward it. As we drew closer I saw the words, 'Procreation Centre' printed in bold letters across the roof. The shuttle slowed, hovered above the parking lot, then the anti-grav clicked off, and we slid into a vacant pod.

The shuttle doors opened. Kane and I stepped out and made our way along a well-marked walkway, through a revolving door, into a large hall. A Robo-receptionist welcomed us. She checked our names and identity chips, punched data into her terminal, produced personalized admittance cards, one for each of us, then escorted us to a room occupied by a distinguished-looking, grey-haired man.

He rose from his desk and held out a hand as we came in. "Welcome and congratulations! It is always a pleasure to meet prospective parents. Allow me to introduce myself. I am Dr. Mendoza, your Genetic Modification Councilor. But, take a seat. Make yourselves comfortable. When you are settled it will be my duty to advise you of all available modifications. We will then record your preferences"

I stared. "Modifications?"

"Genetically modified characteristics. We want to make sure your baby will be adequately equipped to cope with the challenges of the new era."

Kane opened his mouth to reply, but I got in before him. "Thank you, Dr. Mendoza, but we don't want modifications. We just want an ordinary little baby. Isn't that so, Kane?"

Dr. Mendoza's eyebrows shot up, then he leaned back in his chair and regarded me with stern, disapproving eyes. "Do you realize how privileged you are, Mrs. Jackson? Do you know how many couples would give everything they own to change places with you?"

A chill ran through me. The thought that the permit might be withdrawn made me nod, and I stumbled over the words in my haste to answer. "I know. I'm fully aware of that. And we're ever so grateful. I can't tell you how grateful."

He leaned forward and smiled. "Good. Well then, let me to give you some advice. If your pregnancy was allowed to take place haphazardly, without modification and constant supervision, there's a risk the baby might be born with a malformation of some kind. Or mentally impaired. Do you really wish to take that chance?"

This time Kane got in before me. "Of course not. We'll do whatever is necessary to make sure our baby is born whole and healthy." He turned to me. "You agree with that, don't you, Cela?"

I nodded. A malformed baby was the last thing I wanted.

"Very sensible," Dr. Mendoza exclaimed. He punched a button on his keyboard, then looked up and smiled. "We have a new cell-regeneration implant. Would you like me to add that to your list of requirements as well?"

"What effect does it have?" Kane asked.

"It enables the baby to repair damaged cells the moment an injury or infection occurs. It means, in effect, that your child will never get ill, and if injured, will recover in a very short time."

"Sounds good," Kane said. "What do you say, Cela, shall we include that as well?"

I hesitated, and for a moment thought of saying no, but it seemed such a sensible thing to agree to. After all, how could any mother deny her child good health when it was in her power to ensure it? Besides, I was conscious of Dr. Mendoza's eyes on me. "Okay. Put it on the list."

"Now, what about the sex of the child?" Dr. Mendoza asked. "Would you prefer a boy or a girl?"

I didn't mind one way or another and would have preferred to leave it to chance, but Kane's face lit up, and for the first time showed a spark of enthusiasm. "A boy. I would really like a son." He turned to me, brows raised, a question in his eyes. "That's if it's okay with you?"

I shrugged and gave him a smile. "Fine. That's fine with me."

Dr. Mendoza pressed another button, then turned his attention to the next item on his list. "Intelligence. There are various levels to choose from. We don't recommend below average, but you may choose average, above average, superior or genius. Each level is categorized by universally accepted IQ ratings. What is your preference?"

Kane's eyes opened wide. "Do you mean...that if I request it...my son will be a genius? Is that really possible?"

"Most definitely," Dr. Mendoza assured him. "Our geneticists have made wonderful progress in the last few years. Would you like me to add super intelligence to your list of requirements?"

I could feel a headache coming on, a bad one, and there was a strange, high-pitched buzzing in my ears. I wanted to scream, "Stop. Do you hear me? Stop. It's my baby you're talking about, and that's not what I want. That's not what I want at all." But I clenched my jaw and pressed my lips together because Kane's hand reached out to touch mine, and because Dr. Mendoza had turned to stare at me again. I would not give him cause to think I was crazy.

Kane must have taken my silence for agreement, because he answered for both of us. "Definitely. Top of the range intelligence is an absolute must."

The next item on Dr. Mendoza's list was 'Physical Appearance'. He pushed a form across the desk and instructed us to fill in the blanks indicating our choice of hair colour, eye colour, skin tone, as well as a number of other details. After that came, 'Temperament'. And after that, 'Athletic Ability'. There was more, a whole lot more, but by then my mind was reeling and I was finding it difficult to concentrate. Kane, on the other hand, seemed to be enjoying himself. I left it all to him.

Dr. Mendoza smiled as he closed the file. "Now sit back and relax while I go over the procedures that will have to be carried out, step by step, before the infant is delivered."

I could hear his voice, droning on and on, but his words were too technical for me to grasp, and I only caught an odd phrase that made any sense. "...a small operation to harvest the egg ...completely painless ...fertilized in the laboratory ...DNA ...Critical period..." And then at last, "When we are sure the embryo is viable, it will be implanted into Cela's uterus."

"And that's it?" Kane asked.

"Not quite. The baby's development must be monitored very, very carefully. Various medications and stimuli must be applied at specific intervals. It will be necessary for Cela to visit the Centre twice a week for the first three months, three times a week for the next three, and every day for the last trimester."

I frowned. "Stimuli? What kind of stimuli?"

"At first simply recordings of your voice, lullabies, stuff like that, all very soothing."

It was a strange concept, but one I rather liked. "Will the baby be able to hear at such a young age?"

"Oh yes. No doubt about it. And don't forget your infant is destined to be a genius. He will assimilate speech-patterns and comprehend basic mathematics from a very early age."

There was more, something about chemicals and metabolism and the effect of radiation and supersonic sound waves on brain development. Dr. Mendoza must have seen the blank look on my face because he broke off in the middle of a sentence and chuckled softly. "There, that's enough for today. And don't you go worrying about the details. All you have to do is make an appointment with our receptionist and follow instructions. Leave the rest to us. We'll take care of it all for you."

* * * *

The first weeks were the worst. Worrying about whether the embryo would survive kept me awake at night, and the thought I might lose it, and have to go through the whole process all over again, reduced me to tears. But when Dr. Mendoza announced the critical period was over, and all was well, I relaxed and began to enjoy my pregnancy.

Shopping for baby garments and nursery furniture and furnishings, took up a lot of time. There was no shortage of goods to choose from, but most were designed for RoBabies, and the real-wool and real-cotton articles I wanted, were difficult to come across.

I searched the library's archive to find micro-books on motherhood, and read them slowly, one by one. Dr. Mendoza laughed when I told him. He made some remark about old-fashioned ideas, but I didn't care. I enjoyed reading about 'bonding' and 'how to bathe a baby' and a stack of other interesting topics. Photos of red and wrinkled newborns, with tiny fingers and unseeing, milky eyes, brought a lump to my throat. I could hardly wait to hold my own baby in my arms.

Nine months is a long time, but with so much to keep me occupied, the days flew. I spent long hours at the Centre, more often than not wired to a machine that throbbed and pulsed and emitted strange, supersonic vibrations. Now and again I was given a handful of pills and a glass of some strange liquid to swallow.

Dr. Mendoza kept a check on my progress, and week by week, gave encouraging reports. "Fine. You're doing fine." And, "Bonny little fellow you've got in there." When I became impatient and complained about the discomfort, he gave me an encouraging pat on the back. "Nearly there," he said. "Not much longer now."

The sessions at the Centre grew longer and more tedious. I had no idea what it was all about, and didn't like the idea of bombarding the baby with so much stimuli, but when I expressed my concern to Kane, he only laughed. "Relax. Dr. Mendoza knows what he's doing. Leave it to him."

Then, at last there came a day when Dr. Mendoza looked up from his scanner and smiled. "Time's up. Tell Kane to take the day off tomorrow and get you here bright and early. And remember, there's nothing to worry about. The delivery will be quick and painless."

I have no idea what they gave me to drink but it worked like a charm. I went into labour at nine on the dot, and by ten it was all over, no pain, no fuss, no worries, no problems.

Kane held my hand when Dr. Mendoza lifted the baby and held it up for us to see. "Congratulations!" he announced. "You have a fine, bonny son."

I stared, feeling my heart swell with pride as I took in the child's blue eyes, blond curls and peaches-and-cream complexion. Perfect! Absolutely perfect. Everything we'd dreamed of, everything we'd been promised. There was nothing red or wrinkled about this baby. He was as beautiful and flawless as a porcelain doll.

I held out my arms. "Give him to me. Let me hold him. Oh, Kane, isn't he gorgeous?"

Kane squeezed my hand. "You bet, Honey, you bet."

Dr. Mendoza held the child closer. I reached out to take him.

Then the small rosebud mouth opened. Words came out, each as clear and distinct as a bell.

"Mama...Papa...Mama...Papa...Mama...Papa..."

I must have fainted because when I opened my eyes again Dr.

Mendoza was not there. Nor was the baby.

"They've taken him to the nursery," Kane told me. "But he's fine. Dr. Mendoza gave him a thorough going over, and he's assured me the child has every Genetic modification we requested. He's perfect in every way."

Tears welled up and spilled over, way beyond my control. "But...Oh, Kane, he's not like a baby at all," I sobbed. "Not a real one. He's like . . .like . . .a RoBaby."

Kane gave a small, amused laugh. "Yes, in a way I guess he is. But that's great. Just think we won't ever have to worry about him catching a cold, or picking up a bug of any kind." He paused and a thoughtful expression crossed his face. "What are we going to call him? Have you thought of a name?"

"A name?" My head was aching unbearably and my limbs felt numb and icy cold. For a moment I could only stare. Then a name floated into my head, and from far, far away, I heard myself laugh. "Robby. We'll call him Robby. I can't think of a more perfect name."

Kane frowned. "Honey, are you okay?"

I tried to stifle the laughter, but it bubbled up no matter how hard I tried. "Why...why do you ask?"

Kane's frown deepened. "You're acting very strangely. Not like yourself at all."

"I'm fine," I told him. "Absolutely fine."

And I was, because quite suddenly my head stopped thumping, and I knew everything was going to be okay. More than okay, because I had it all worked out. On our way home from the Proc-Centre we would stop by at the RoBaby factory. And then...and then we would trade Robby in. For a girl. Yes...a girl would be nice. A girl with big brown eyes and dark hair like mine. A girl-baby who would cry. And cry. . .and cry. . .and cry. . .

The End

About the Author

Daphne Olivier grew up in the foothills of the Amatolas, where the novel is set, and where many of the locals still speak with pride of their German/Irish heritage. The story of the Kennaway Girls has always fascinated her, and a visit to the museum in East London, which displays a collection of historic memorabilia, inspired her to write a novel based on the life of one of these brave women.

After training as a nurse, Daphne married and for many years lived on a farm. Today she lives in a small South African town together with her husband and their two dogs.

Email: dafol@mtnloaded.co.za

Other works by the author with Melange Books

The Kennaway Woman
The Way it Was

Imari Jade ~ Daphne Olivier ~ Tori L. Ridgewood ~ Joanne Rawson

Tabitha's Solution

by

Tori L. Ridgewood

Tabitha's Solution
Tori L. Ridgewood

February 6, 2001

He was nearly a week overdue.

Tabitha traced the red circle she had drawn on the calendar to mark her due date six and a half months earlier.

"Time to come out, little one," she murmured, patting her full, round belly. The burden inside shifted lazily under her touch. "Just try not to hurt mama too much on the way, all right?"

In twenty-four hours, if things didn't get moving on their own, her labour would have to be induced. Tabitha was more than ready to get going, but the prospect of that particular medical procedure somehow bothered her more than the idea of giving birth itself. Her body would know what to do when the time came. Having extra poking and prodding to make it happen seemed a little like—overkill.

But her midwife had been adamant: if she was not in labour by the 7th, away to the hospital they would go. No home birth. Possibly a c-section.

It seemed like her pregnancy could be summed up in numbers.

Six and a half days overdue.

Two years of trying. Less than some parents experienced, but longer than others would tolerate before heading to the fertility doctor.

Eight pregnancy tests before her husband, Alex, was assured that they were really and truly going to have a baby. He'd been thrilled after the two little blue lines appeared in the first test, but he'd suggested that she pee on the stick again, and again, and again, just in case. After all, the second test had shown negative results. Later, at the midwives' office, they'd learned that a false negative was a common phenomenon in the early stages.

There was no doubt about it at this point, Tabitha reflected. The negative had definitely been false.

Forty pounds of extra weight...please let it come off quickly, she prayed.

Tabitha wrenched her gaze away from the calendar as the kettle shrieked on the stove. She padded heavily over to turn off the element, not quite waddling but not in an easy gait. Since her pelvis had loosened a few weeks ago, walking was a bit of an adventure in balance. Her great, round belly made her feel like a cow at times, unwieldy and awkward. In other moments, when she caught a glimpse of her silhouette with her full breasts and plump bottom, and her hair grown out longer than it had ever been, she felt deliciously womanly and sexy.

An opinion that Alex was happy to share.

"Hey, gorgeous," he called out from the top of the stairs to their basement apartment, "I rented you a movie for tonight!"

The sound of the door shutting echoed down the stairs. Tabitha smiled tiredly. No matter how fat and exhausted she became, her husband never failed to make her feel better. She listened to him coming in, tromping down the plastic liner on the carpet.

"Shoes!" she reminded him, without turning.

"Shoes," Alex grudgingly agreed, grumbling cheerfully as he turned back to the bottom steps.

Every speck of dirt showed in their tiny wall-to-wall cream carpet one-bedroom basement apartment. Organization seemed to be the one goal that consistently escaped Tabitha's grasp. There were copious piles of textbooks, binders, bills, used tea mugs, and discarded notes on every flat surface, marking her as a university student in her final year. The bright, open-concept main room had enough space for their kitchen table, two second-hand couches, the coffee table, her overcrowded plywood computer desk, a cheap wooden shelf for the stereo, their cable-less TV, and the cheap VCR they had purchased, on sale, instead of the expensive new DVD player they had wanted. A large fruitless orange tree, the only plant that Tabitha had managed to avoid killing with love, marked the boundary between the living space and eating space.

She called the plant "George".

Tabitha's inability to keep green things alive didn't bother her as much as the clutter in their home. Alex never complained that they couldn't actually eat at the table. The worn-in sofa cushions were fine, he reassured her; the baby certainly wouldn't care. She plunked a decaffeinated tea bag in her mug, eying the piles of clean laundry in the middle of the room that still needed folding. Her husband's clean aprons and chef's coats lay precariously on top of the largest pile, taunting her. She couldn't procrastinate on the housework anymore, having finished her last essay for the term that morning. At least, with the baby so overdue, she had been able to complete her final assignments and would be awarded her degree. That was one worry she could finally put aside.

But the mess...If their home was going to be ready for the little stranger, she had to get busy after he changed and went to his second shift of the day. Alex did what he could to contribute, washing dishes, making meals ahead, and doing all the grocery shopping in the knowledge that Tabitha loathed those chores, but he had been working extra shifts for months to put extra money aside.

Who knew? Maybe a round of energetic cleaning would get things in the uterine department moving!

Alex, his shoes left on the plastic, held the video up as he came toward her. "I feel bad, you're all alone these days."

She set the mug on the counter and pressed herself into him, enjoying the close embrace. "It's all right. I'm worried more about you. You're working too hard."

He kissed the top of her head. "I'm fine. I get enough sleep for now. After the baby comes, I probably won't. I'll take what I can get at the moment."

"I feel like it's my fault that this is taking so long," Tabitha confessed. "I've tried everything."

He stroked her cheek. "It's not your fault. She's just really comfortable in there. I don't blame her for wanting to stay."

"Do you wish we had found out for sure?" She looked up at him, searching for reassurance. "Whether it's a boy or a girl?"

"Nope." Alex cupped her face in his hands and kissed her. "It's the best surprise we're ever going to have."

* * * *

Eight days earlier, Tabitha had been absolutely positive that the baby was on her way. Her entire pregnancy had been incident-free: no morning sickness, no swollen ankles, no varicose veins. A few stretch marks now crossed her abdomen, but otherwise it had been text-book perfect.

"I'm so excited, I just know it's going to go smoothly, Mom." Tabitha grinned as she cradled the phone between her chin and shoulder. The soft pastel green receiving blanket she was folding crackled with static electricity in her hands as she shook out the fold. "Plus, if we do have the baby tomorrow—no, when we have the baby tomorrow, I'm going to think positively—I'll win that brand-new nursery at the mall!"

"But you already have a crib, and a stroller."

"I couldn't resist entering that contest. I just had a really good feeling about it." Tabitha added the tidy square of fabric to the linen shelf beside the crib, and picked up a cotton one printed with yellow duckies. "It includes a bassinet with a lacy lining, so Victorian and adorable, plus a changing table. I don't have a changing table."

"Do you really have room for all of that?" Her mother cautioned. "We talked about that. Until you move, you're pretty crowded as it is. That's why I got you that rail-riding changing thingy."

Tabitha suppressed a sigh. "I'd make it work, Mom. I'm creative. I play Tetris, I like rearranging things." She refused to look around again at the small bedroom holding the old double-bed, one long dresser, a side table with a lamp, and for the baby, the linen shelf she had converted from an old plant stand. The crib was squeezed into the only space left, nearly blocking the bedroom door.

"I wish I could be down there with you, dear," her mother sighed.

"I know. I do too." Tabitha hoped she sounded sincere. On the one hand, having her mother present during her labour would be a comfort. On the other, she wasn't entirely comfortable with the idea. It was going to be hard enough being exposed to the midwives again! Tabitha never even let women in a change room see her naked, always putting on her swimsuit in the bathroom.

Still, she had imagined her mom waiting just outside the delivery room, and being one of the first to hold her new grandchild. That would have been wonderful.

"Did your washer and dryer ever come?" her mom asked.

"Yes, just yesterday." With great relish, Tabitha described her new appliances as though they were toys. "They're really shiny, Mom. So much better than going to the laundromat. I can't believe we lucked out on an apartment with a laundry room, let alone that we were able to buy the set on sale. It's going to make using cloth diapers much easier."

Tabitha didn't care that her mother was probably rolling her eyes. This was a debate she had often gotten into with her. No, she did care. "I know you think it's silly, but it's really better for the environment."

"All you're doing is using more electricity," her mother argued. "Why else did they invent disposables? God knows, if they had had disposables when you and your brother were babies..."

"There are mothers in India who never put their babies in diapers," Tabitha pointed out. "Babies have survived being put in cloth diapers for thousands of years. It'll help him to toilet train faster, if he feels the wet."

"Tabitha. This is a baby. You're looking at two years before that's even close to happening."

"Yeah, well... I want to try it, anyway. And I know there are moms out there who have potty trained their babies at thirteen months." A lump pushed at her hand, to the left of her navel. It was most likely a foot. She prodded it back, and the foot abruptly struck her lower rib. "Ow. Besides, it's a lot easier than it used to be, with Kushies that have Velcro tabs instead of pins."

Tabitha knew she'd never be able to convince her mom.

"When will Dad be back from his business trip?"

"Oh, in about a week." The tone of her mother's voice changed from wistful to bemused. "He's been trying to get me to fly out and join him in Vancouver, but I'd rather be closer to you. Maybe I should take the train down, what do you think about that?"

"Mom, you'd have to sleep on our couch. It's just not practical." Not to mention the single bathroom they'd have to share! "I'll be fine. I can take care of a baby."

"Mm-hmm."

"Really, it's going to be great!"

"Okay."

"I mean, Alex is going to take a few days off, and the midwives will be doing two home visits, so I won't be completely alone. I can take care of the baby."

"What about the rabbit?"

Tabitha glanced down at the black-and-white German bunny sniffing around her feet. "I can take care of Beatrice too. She can run around while I'm feeding the baby. She won't be a problem. We finally got her litter-trained, so cleaning the cage is easier, too."

"Well, if you need me to take her, let me know."

"It's fine, Mom." Tabitha cringed. She didn't want to sound like a whiny teenager. "Listen, I have to go to the bathroom. I just got kicked in the bladder again. I'll call you first thing tomorrow, and as soon as my labour starts, all right?"

"I love you, Tabby-cat."

"Love you, too."

Tabitha rubbed her belly as she set the phone back in its cradle. "Your grandmamma is going to love you solo much, little one," she reflected aloud. "We just have to be patient a little while longer. It would be nice for her to be here, but we just don't have the space! I've read all the books. I know how to take care of you. How hard can it be? You're just one little baby."

Her bump shifted abruptly, as though in response.

"Yes, yes, I get it. My poor bladder is crowding you. Well, let's take care of that." Quickly folding the last three blankets and setting them on the shelf, Tabitha grabbed her battered copy of What To Expect When You're Expecting, and headed to the bathroom. She emerged, a short time later, feeling slightly disgruntled.

Where were all the signs of imminent labour? Her muscles had been scrunching and relaxing inconsistently for a week, a strange but not unpleasant sensation, but there had been no pain to suggest that it was time. Sherry, her primary caregiver, had said that she was experiencing pre-labour, and that it was a good thing. But nothing else had happened.

No bloody show. She wasn't quite sure what that would be like, in spite of the book's description.

No sudden gushes of fluid, or flare-ups of back pain, not that she really wanted to experience these things. Tabitha just wanted to have her baby, as quickly as possible. If it was at all possible, it would be ideal to avoid involving needles. It wouldn't be comfortable, but unless medical intervention was absolutely necessary, no needles would come anywhere near her skin.

Admittedly, all the battle stories she'd heard from her prenatal classes, and read in her books, about the potential side effects of drugs on a baby's brain—or on the mother, so she couldn't remember giving birth—had strengthened her prejudice against modern medicine. Plus, the fact that even watching someone getting a needle made her nauseous. Therefore getting an epidermal was completely out of the question. Absolutely nobody was getting near her spine with a sharp object unless she was knocked out, first.

Punctured spinal column. Tabitha shuddered at the thought.

Alex was completely on her side. He attended as many appointments with her as he could, and understood her fears. "I won't let anyone touch you, unless there's a problem," he promised her, over and over.

She was relying on that.

Her mother had reminisced often enough about Tabitha's own introduction to the world. In 1977, women had had to shave when they went into labour, and then have an enema. Ick. Thank goodness hospitals in Ontario no longer did any of that. Tabitha did not relish the picture her mother had painted of a woman who had just given birth running to the toilet. Sherry had laid those fears to rest in one of her early appointments.

"Enemas? No, no, that's not done anymore," she shook her head, smiling. "And you'll only need a catheter if you go in for a c-section. We'll cross that bridge when we come to it. If there is a problem, we'll refer you right away to the obstetrician-gynecologist."

"How quickly could the OB-GYN get there, if the baby's in distress?" Alex knew all the terminology, from his years as a volunteer with the St. John Ambulance. He smiled at Tabitha, squeezing her hand as tightly as she held his own.

"He'll be either in the hospital, or on-call, depending on how you are at the beginning of your labour." Sherry consulted a schedule hanging on the wall. Her light brown curly hair reminded Tabitha of her mother. "In fact, the doctor has a couple of scheduled inductions and a caesarean booked around your due date. I don't think you'll need to worry, unless the baby is breech or something else is going on."

So many things could go wrong, but Tabitha tried not to think about that. For over eight months, ever since she had confirmed that she was pregnant, she was only ever optimistic that her first birth would be perfect. Traditional, in the modern sense. She would breathe through the pains, using her meditation and yoga training. She would visualize, to help her body relax. She would have her favourite soft-rocks or new age music playing, and a scented candle. They would be in the hospital, just in case, but Alex would be by her side through the whole experience and make sure that it was just like she wanted.

Perfect.

Twenty-four more hours, and she would be a mother. Alex would be a dad. All of this discomfort and concern would be behind them.

* * * *

Thirty-six hours later, Tabitha had to stop herself from grinding her teeth with impatience.

"Honey, what are you doing with that shovel?"

Tabitha huffed and puffed, her breath coming in little clouds of condensation. "What does it look like I'm doing? I'm shoveling."

Alex approached her with the caution of a bomb defuser approaching an unknown container. "I can see that. But sweetheart, you're nine months pregnant. Why don't you let me do that?"

She glared at him over her muffler, without breaking her rhythm. "I'm fine. It's just a couple of inches of snow."

"Then why are you out here?" He gestured helplessly.

"I'm trying to get this baby moving!" Tabitha bent at the knees, forcing the blade of the shovel under a crust of snow by the walkway to their door. The couple who lived in the main floor of the one-story house had already offered to salt the concrete paving stones, but Tabitha had graciously declined. "I figured, if I do a little bending, and lifting, maybe it would get my water to break or something."

"O...kay...then..."

She saw his hesitation and skepticism, and sighed. "I missed out on the damned draw, all right? I'm pissed off, and pregnant, and overdue, and I want to have this baby!"

Alex held up his hands. "Hey, I respect that. I'm just trying to help."

Tabitha swallowed her crankiness. She tried to smile. "You can help by moving, dearest."

Obediently stepping to the left, Alex watched her attack the next section of sidewalk. "I brought you home some rotisserie chicken, with mashed potatoes."

She didn't stop moving. "Super. Go ahead and plate it, I'll be down

107

in about five or ten minutes."

"Do you want a cup of tea?"

"I'd really love a martini, dirty. But I guess tea will have to do." Tabitha relented as soon as the words were out of her mouth. Dropping the shovel, she threw her arms around her husband, stretching to accommodate their winter coats. "I'm sorry, I'm just in a bitch."

"It's fine, I understand." Alex rubbed the small of her back, in just the place she liked. She made an appreciative noise, and he continued, "I mean, I sort of get it. You're tired, and frustrated. We'll get there soon. But you really don't need to be out here."

"I promise, I'll come down just as soon as I get this path cleared." She released him and thrust her belly forward. "This baby is coming out tonight!"

* * * *

Tabitha scanned the choices under the glass at the Jumping Bean. Three days past her due date, she had called up Sam, her study partner and best friend, for lunch. The mall was busy, and a line of shoppers waited impatiently behind her, but her body was so hugely pregnant that nobody dared question her.

"Hurry up, Tab."

Nobody, except her friend Sam, who was waiting at the register with her own tray of corn chips, salsa, and garden salad already paid for.

"Give me a number three, and a four, and a seven," she ordered, tapping the sneeze guard. "What else do you have that's super-spicy?"

"Geez Louise, you're going to end up with heartburn until tomorrow," Sam told her as they headed to a table.

"I can deal with heartburn," Tabitha replied grimly, edging around a shopping cart left inconveniently in the aisle. "I've been dealing with heartburn since the second trimester. But I heard that spicy food can make labour start, so I'm loading up."

Sam raised her eyebrows. "Really? I didn't know that."

Tabitha shrugged. "Hey, at this point, I'm willing to try anything."

"Didn't that girl in your prenatal class drink a whole jar of hot pepper juice?"

"Pickled hot pepper juice," Tabitha amended. "But yeah, after eating all the peppers. Why?"

"Did that make her go into labour?"

Tabitha's eyes were watering from the extra-hot jalapeno peppers she'd asked for on her taco. She had to gulp some chocolate milk before her throat would relax enough to answer, "No, but Jaya always ate spicy foods. I hardly ever do, so there you go."

"How do you know she always eats spicy foods?" Sam narrowed her eyes at Tabitha over her loaded tortilla.

"Are you trying to piss off the pregnant woman?" Tabitha smiled sweetly, showing all of her teeth. "Because right now, I could cheerfully eat you with enough hot sauce."

"I'm just saying…"

"Jaya and I were in the same introductory psych class, and we had study meetings with food. Anyone with a yen for hot and spicy just had to ask her. She had East Indian recipes out the yang."

"Have you seen her lately?"

Tabitha shook her head. "Not since she had her own baby last year. She finished the course, but it was hard on her."

Sam picked at her salad. "It's going to be hard on you, too."

"I know, but I have Alex. It'll be fine. At least this is my last year, and I'll be working in a few months." Tabitha straightened her shoulders as much as she could with the weight of her belly, and gamely stuffed her mouth with another bite of nuclear taco. She watched her friend shake with silent laughter as her face turned red.

"So what will you do if the spicy food doesn't work?"

Wagging at a finger at the tall redhead across the table, Tabitha chugged the rest of her drink. "Don't jinx me! It's going to work!" she gasped, trying to hold back a belch and failing. "Excuse me. As much as I love carrying this child, I will be so happy to have my body back. I may not end up the same size --"

"My mom's friend, Sandi, walked out of the hospital in the same jeans she wore to her first prenatal appointment. After giving birth to twins." Sam gestured with her fork toward Tabitha's beach-ball-sized stomach.

"—but at least I won't have someone constantly kicking me in the gut. And yes, I've heard the Sandi story before, thanks for reminding me." Tabitha shook her head in disgust. "I still don't believe it."

* * * *

The morning of the fifth day after zero hour dawned bright and beautiful.

The bottle of mineral oil sat on the bathroom counter, gleaming under the row of incandescent bulbs lining the mirror.

Tabitha sat on the edge of the bathtub, looking at it.

Her massive belly quivered as the full-grown, invisible fetus tried to turn over inside her.

It was supposed to be a natural laxative, but Tabitha didn't know if she had the courage to take it. The Mexican food had been bad enough. And still, no baby.

"Tab? Do you need any help in there?"

Tabitha closed her eyes and clenched her fists on the porcelain. "No, I'm fine. I'll be out in a minute."

He probably thought things were starting. She wished she could tell him it was happening. Opening her eyes again, she reached across the short distance and picked up the clear plastic bottle to read the instructions once more.

"I've got a surprise for you out here." Alex called through the door.

Resigned, Tabitha slowly and awkwardly got to her feet and put the mineral oil back in the cupboard.

In the living room, Alex was standing with his hands behind his back, beaming. "I got you something, and you'll never guess what it is. You were so sound asleep last night when I got home, I didn't want to wake you up, but I guarantee that you'll love it."

She had to grin, despite her weariness. "Can you give me a hint?"

Her husband whistled a few bars of a song.

Tabitha clasped her hands with delight. "You rented Babe?"

"Even better." Alex presented her with a VHS tape, flourishing it proudly. "I bought you your very own copy. I wish I could have gotten you the DVD and a player to go with it, but they'll be cheaper in a couple of years."

"That's wonderful!" Tabitha gushed, moving forward in an awkward pregnant rush. "Thank you so much! Now I can learn the lullaby that the farmer sings to the pig. That sounds so stupid when I say it out loud, but it really is such a nice song."

He embraced her gently. "How are you feeling?"

Tabitha leaned her head against his shoulder, setting the movie on the back of the couch. "Huge. Exhausted. Nervous."

Alex nibbled her ear. "It'll be over soon, sweetheart. You've got your appointment in two days, and if they have to induce you, so be it. Maybe you'll go into labour tonight. You never know. Maybe by tomorrow night, we'll have our baby."

"I'm so tired of being pregnant," Tabitha moaned, clasping her hands around his neck. She rose on her toes to kiss his lips. "I'm very happy, and I know I'll miss this. But it needs to be over."

He chuckled, kneading her lower back. He pressed lightly, encouraging her to put her weight against him for a moment. "Do you remember when we sent the picture of the last pregnancy test to your parents?"

Tabitha turned her face to the side, grinning. "They thought it was a weird design for a ceiling fan." Without warning, her eyes brimmed over. "I really wanted them to be here."

Alex was patient, as always, while she cried out her tension. He rocked her gently. "We could always try jumping up and down."

Laughing through her tears, Tabitha nodded. Alex held her tightly and jiggled her, lifting her feet from the floor.

"Stop, stop! You'll make me pee myself!" She shrieked with laughter as he pulled her higher. "Here, I'll do it!"

Alex let her go.

Tabitha jumped.

"No, no. You need some music!" He moved to the stereo and put on a dance CD.

Laughing, Tabitha bounced around the room, holding her belly with both hands. "I feel ridiculous!"

Alex was tapping his foot to the beat. "Want to stop?"

She was determined to go as long as her lungs and her legs would allow. "Never!"

"What if the baby gets seasick?" Alex arched an eyebrow at her.

"Oh, come on," Tabitha scoffed. "This is nothing. I went to the mall the other day, took a bumpy road, and I went slowly. The suspension on the car is okay, by the way," she reassured him. "But that was a rocking ride, and nothing. No baby."

Alex brought her a glass of water when her energy finally gave out.

"Look at it this way," he offered, "We're getting some extra sleep. Bonus nights that we'll miss later."

"Maybe," Tabitha gasped, wiping the beads of sweat from her forehead. "Or maybe I just got things started!"

* * * *

At present, six and a half days after her baby was supposed to be in her arms, Tabitha was taking out her frustrations on the house. Hands that should have been stroking an infant's petal-soft cheeks and diapering a tiny bum were rinsing sponges and dusting cupboards with furious energy.

It was late for nesting, but there was nothing else to do.

The crib was still empty.

The stack of diapers on the linen shelf was gathering lint.

The rabbit hopped impatiently back and forth in her cage as Tabitha quickly swept and mopped the floor.

"I know, I know, Beatrice." Tabitha dipped the mop in the bucket with such force that dirty water sloshed over the side. "Oh, crap. You'll just have to be patient, bunny."

After one more swipe to clean up the excess, the kitchen was done. With one hand supporting the underside of her belly, Tabitha reached down to pick up the bucket.

A strong, masculine hand covered hers.

"It's all right, sweetheart. Let me do that."

Tabitha let Alex help her straighten up. She leaned against the kitchen counter as he carried the bucket into the laundry room.

When he came back out, he was carrying a bouquet of roses.

"How did you sneak those in here?" Tabitha felt giddy. She buried her grin in the flowers when he handed them to her.

"Oh, I have my ways." Alex led her to the couch, and after she sat, he eased down next to her, holding her feet on his lap. "I was going to wait until after the baby's born, but I know you've been tired and frustrated. I'll get you more after she's born."

Tabitha laughed. "You're always so certain it's a girl."

"Well, after he's born, then." Alex rubbed the arch of her foot. "You know I don't care, as long as the baby's healthy."

"It's definitely healthy," Tabitha muttered, drawing the soft, velvety petals of the roses under her chin. "Wiggling around and kicking at me all the time. I'm black and blue on the inside. This morning, I could swear I got pinched!"

"Remember when we read that you're not supposed to rub a pregnant woman's feet?" Alex slowly pulled off both of her socks, dropping them on the floor. "There's a nerve in there that might cause contractions to start, supposedly."

Tabitha relaxed against the back and arm of the sofa. "If that's an offer for a massage, I'm definitely for it."

"Want to watch a movie, too?"

"That would be nice."

Alex moved with casual assurance, setting up the tape and bringing a vase for the flowers. By the time he sat back down to take Tabitha's feet back into his lap, she had a glass of milk by her elbow, a plate of cookies, and a throw draped across her body.

"I love you," she sighed, as he moulded his hands to her feet.

"I love you, too."

The movie he put in was one of her many favourites, a romantic comedy. After a while, she closed her eyes and just listened while he kneaded and rubbed the tired muscles forming the ball of her foot. Gently, so she wouldn't flinch with the tickle, he manipulated each toe. Her body relaxed even further when he rotated first one heel, and then the other, loosening the joint. His hands were very warm, and soft on her skin, though slightly scarred and calloused from working with chef's knives.

* * * *

"Tabby."

Drowsy, and too comfortable to move, Tabitha tried to roll more deeply into the corner of the couch.

"Come on, honey. I know you're tired, but you've got to come to bed."

Groaning, Tabitha let him pull her up to a sitting position. "I was so relaxed. I could have slept out here."

"Yes, but I would miss you." Alex kissed her hands.

A warmth spread throughout her body at the touch of his lips. "You know, there's something else I learned while I was reading this week. Another way to induce labour."

She got to her feet, putting her weight on Alex's arms as his hands grasped her elbows. The love in his eyes washed over her. "What is it?"

She licked her lips. "The basic ingredients in pitocin are essentially the same as what's in sperm. Not very romantic, I know." Her voice was hushed. "And I know I'm not very attractive right now, but—"

Her words were stopped by his mouth on her own.

"I think you're very sexy, and you always are," he murmured, drawing her with him to the bedroom. "With your round breasts, and our child in your belly. How could I not want you?"

* * * *

Spooning under the covers, Tabitha stroked Alex's hand as it rested on the upper curve of her abdomen.

"I wonder what he thought of that?" he whispered into her hair.

She laughed, feeling her belly shake.

"Well, it was probably like a roller-coaster ride or something. At the very least, the tilt-a-whirl." She squeezed his fingers and nestled her bottom more firmly against him.

"Is that rain?" Alex turned his head away for a moment. "It sounds like rain."

"In February?"

"Sounds like it." He kissed the side of her neck, before slipping out of the bed. "Hang on a second. I'll be right back for more cuddling."

He paused to put on a pair of sweatpants, and then quickly went up the stairs.

Tabitha must have drifted off again. The next thing she knew, his icy chin was pressing under her earlobe.

"Hey!"

"Sorry, but you're so warm."

"What were you doing?" she muttered plaintively. "Rolling in the snow?"

"I had to lift the windshield wipers," he whispered, pulling her closer to him. She didn't protest again. Her body had been like a furnace for months. "It's freezing rain out there. It will not be nice, chipping the ice off the glass in the morning. I'll have to salt the drive as soon as I get up."

"Um," said Tabitha. She was already, once again, drifting.

* * * *

The windows in their small, modern, basement apartment were not large, but the bright walls helped to spread any light that came in. While Alex liked it as dark as possible, Tabitha often left the curtains open to catch the early morning sun. It was nice to open her eyes to the light streaming in from the east.

But this time, Tabitha wasn't certain what had awoken her. The light outside was grey, showing that the sun was barely up, or that it was extremely cloudy. She didn't bother to look at the clock, needing to use the bathroom so badly there was a dull ache in the bottom of her abdomen.

114

Her grogginess vanished when she saw what was on the tissue.

Smiling widely, she crawled back into the bed beside her husband. "We're going to have a baby today," she told him, softly.

Alex gathered her into his arms. "Okay," he yawned. "Do you want to call the midwife?"

She checked the clock. "It's six-thirty," she answered. "I'm not feeling any pain yet, just cramping a little. Maybe we should wait."

They lay, talking quietly, for forty minutes. Tabitha became acutely aware that the cramp in her lower belly had taken on a rhythmic quality. It ebbed and fell in waves, not unlike an earache. Still, it wasn't terribly uncomfortable.

Finally, at seven-thirty, she made the call.

"I'm so sorry, did I wake you?"

"No, no, I was up." Sherry sounded sleepy, but cheerful. "Are you having contractions?"

"Yes, I think so." Tabitha's enthusiasm bubbled over as she described her sensations. "Should I go to the hospital?"

"Well, by the sounds of it, you've still got a while yet. It's good that your contractions are regular, but they're about ten or fifteen minutes apart, right?" Tabitha could hear children's voices in the background, as Sherry's own family began their day. "You have an appointment scheduled this morning at eleven, so why don't you come in then and we'll have a look?"

A bit disappointed, Tabitha agreed. In the next moment, another wave of squeezing cramp swept away her misgivings. Clearly, it was going to happen, in only a matter of hours.

"Thank goodness for small miracles," she told Alex, after she hung up the phone. "Now I don't have to worry about being induced!"

With time to kill before her appointment, Tabitha wandered the apartment after Alex went to work, knowing he was only a phone call away. She did a few final loads of laundry after breakfast. She paused to rest when she felt the pains, which were really only as bad as period cramps, and started reading Gone with the Wind again to take her mind off things. Then, at ten-thirty, she put on her coat, grabbed her purse and car keys, and slowly made her way up the stairs with one hand firmly gripping the rail.

Outside, the freezing rain had warmed into a tepid sleet. Alex had thoughtfully scattered extra salt on the porch, stairs, and walkway. Still, she shuffled her way down to the car.

"It's as bad as Christmas Eve when you're a kid," she muttered to herself. Alex had also scraped her windshield, but she had to wait for the engine to warm up. "What else do I have to wait for, today?"

Maybe if Tabitha hadn't spoken the words aloud, she wouldn't have run into the construction detour.

Or gotten behind the city bus.

By the time she parked the car at the midwives' office, she was nearly twenty minutes behind schedule. Her belly squeezed as she unclipped the seatbelt. The cramp was stronger, this time.

Sherry wasn't in the office yet, but Tabitha's second midwife, Aidie, was pleasant and gentle as she performed the examination.

"Congratulations! You're at five centimeters!" Aidie patted her foot.

Tabitha exhaled. "Wow. Still a while to go, then."

"You're doing great. Just go home, keep an eye on the time, and call me or Sherry if your water breaks, or when the contractions are five minutes apart."

* * * *

Not willing to go home just yet, to sit and wait alone, Tabitha headed to the local shopping centre, instead.

The mall wasn't busy. Tabitha paced the food court, trying to decide what to order while waiting for Sam to arrive.

"You don't look like you're in labour."

Tabitha turned around. Sam was holding a camera. "Say cheese!"

"No!" Her reaction time was too slow; Sam snapped the picture before Tabitha could get her hand up. "What are you doing? I'm going to have this baby any minute! For real, this time!"

"I'm recording the moment for posterity." Her friend grinned while tucking the camera safely in her bag. "Okay, now, is it time to push yet?"

The dull ache in Tabitha's abdomen wasn't quite going away between the sporadic moments of squeezing discomfort. "No, but I really need to sit down."

"Do you want anything?" Sam's expression softened. She took Tabitha by the hand and pulled her over to a chair. "Let me get you a drink or something. Are you allowed to eat?"

"Actually, I could really go for a slushy," Tabitha admitted. "I feel kind of warm."

"Your face does look a bit red. I'll get it for you."

"Lemonade, please. And maybe a baked potato, with sour cream and chives." The delicious odour coming from the nearby Swiss Chalet was making Tabitha's mouth water.

"You know we have a bet going in the study group," Sam called over from the register as she paid for the food. "If you have the baby anytime between six and ten tonight, I will win fifty dollars!"

"Oh, yeah?" Tabitha leaned back in her chair, wincing. "I will do my best. I've said it before, and I will say it again: I am ready to get this done."

The potato was the best thing she'd ever eaten. Sam got her a refill on the lemonade, and then Tabitha headed home.

Around the construction detour.

And behind a little old lady in a massive Lincoln driving five miles per hour under the speed limit.

* * * *

The remains of supper—another rotisserie chicken, creamed corn, and baked french fries with gravy—sat on the counter while Tabitha took a shower and Alex watched a movie.

The hot water felt wonderfully good on her lower back, while an invisible hand pressed in on her stomach with increasing intensity.

She remembered that the girl from her prenatal class had had her water break while in the shower. Tabitha had no such luck, though. She stood under the massaging spray until the heat faded, and her fingers were wrinkled.

The next cramp made her bottom feel like it was going to fall out. Half dressed, Tabitha sat down, expecting for the normal process, but her water wasn't the only thing refusing to find the exit. She strained for a moment, waiting to see whether her bladder was going to empty or not, hoping for some relief.

The reality dawned on her, quite quickly.

"Alex! I think you should start timing me," she called out, pulling on a pair of drawstring sweatpants.

Alex was crouched in front of the VCR when she emerged, a moment later. "Really? From the beginning of contractions, or the end of each one?"

She breathed out slowly, grabbed a chair from the kitchen table, and reversed it so she could straddle the seat. "I don't remember, just time

117

me."

The feeling of pressure was still there, and the red-hot ache had ramped up a degree or two. She eased back on the chair, so her lower abdomen was no longer touching the wood. Within a few minutes, the crushing need to bear down returned. It quickly strengthened. "I've got another one!" Tabitha gasped. She concentrated on breathing through it.

Across the room, Alex's movie started.

"Zombies, Alex? Seriously?"

"Did that one finish?" He was looking at his watch, grinning sheepishly. "You like zombies, it's for you."

She shook her head with disbelief. "Yes, this one is done. I need some water, please."

In the middle of her sip from the tall glass he handed her, the next contraction began. She gave the glass back to her husband so her hands were free to grip the sides of the chair.

"It just...feels like...I really need...to go to the bathroom," she finished in a rush, huffing and puffing between each word. She leaned her chin on the top rung.

Alex picked up the phone. "Maybe I should call the midwife now."

Tabitha nodded. "Sounds...like...a...plan." She wiped some sweat from her forehead with the edge of her sleeve. "Whew, that one was harder."

It was seven o'clock.

"It's ringing, honey." Alex moved across to turn down the volume on the TV. "Hi, Sherry? Tab thinks it's time. Her contractions are about two or three minutes apart, but we're not sure... Yes, she can talk." Alex held the cordless out so Tabitha could take it.

"Hi...Sherry..." Tabitha smiled, though her lower body now felt like it was burning. She tried to speak confidently, but couldn't help panting. "It...feels...like...I...need...to...   Well,   I   tried   going...to   the bathroom...but...nothing…happened. I had a shower, though."

Finally, after answering a few more questions, Tabitha gave the handset back to Alex. Another wave of pain rendered her speechless. It was so powerful, her ears rang and her vision blurred.

When she could see again, Alex was kneeling in front of her, holding the glass of water.

"She's on her way. She said she usually likes to talk as a diagnostic tool. If you weren't really in labour, she would have heard it in your breathing. I mean, she could tell you were in hard labour because of your breathing. Anyway, she's coming. Have a drink, honey."

Tabitha drank. "Can you call my mother?" she coughed, closing her eyes against the next contraction.

* * * *

By the time Sherry knocked on the door, the interval between Tabitha's pains was down to seconds. She smiled at the older woman as Sherry came down the stairs, black bag in hand. Tabitha's face felt red, her heart was pounding, and her lungs bursting, as though she was running a marathon in the summer instead of sitting backwards on a ladder-back chair in a basement apartment, having a baby.

"Okay, sweetheart, let's have a look at you." Sherry moved to the bedroom behind Tabitha. She heard rustling as the midwife spread a plastic sheet under a soft blanket. A gentle hand came under her arm, helping Tabitha to stand. "I just need to see how much you've dilated."

The examination hurt, even though the midwife was careful. "Ooh, ouch."

"Sorry, Tabitha. You're almost completely effaced, at ten centimeters." Sherry removed her moistened glove. "I bet if I broke that water for you, that last bit of cervix would simply melt away. You'd have your baby in ten or fifteen minutes."

"No," Tabitha shook her head. "No, I want it...to happen...on its own."

"No problem." Sherry helped Tabitha put her garments back together. "Now, here's the question you need to consider: Do you want to stay here? I have all the equipment I need in the trunk of my car. I can put the paramedics on standby. If you were to drive to the hospital now, there's the possibility that the baby will crown and I'd have to help you deliver on the road, in the backseat. If there is a complication, the OB-GYN would arrive at the hospital at approximately the same time that the paramedics would bring you, because you're at relatively the same distance. Plus, it's freezing rain again, so the roads are a bit treacherous. So what do you want to do? Would you prefer to go to the hospital, as planned? Or stay here?"

Tabitha looked over Sherry's shoulder at her husband. Alex nodded at her.

"It's probably better to go to the hospital, right?"

"It's whatever you are comfortable doing, dear."

119

"Let's go to the hospital."

Alex moved forward and helped Sherry raise Tabitha from the bed. The sensation that her bottom was falling out returned. She moved with excruciating slowness, concentrating on putting one foot in front of the other, as another wave of pain and pressure squeezed her middle. Supported by Sherry on one side, Tabitha carefully stepped into her boots after Alex put each one in front of her. He put her coat on her shoulders and helped her slide her arms into the sleeves.

Tabitha raised her eyes to the stairs.

The run of sixteen-odd steps had never seemed unusually high, or steep. Through the glass door, the ice-lined branches of a tree near their driveway were thrashing in a nasty wind. Tabitha could see beads of ice hitting the glass and freezing.

A series of frightening images ran through Tabitha's mind.

What if she was halfway up the stairs, and suddenly, whoosh— amniotic fluid everywhere? Would Alex and Sherry be able to get her back down?

What if the baby started crowning while she was in the back of the car? Did she want to end up on the evening news?

"Can I change my mind?"

Alex kissed her cheek. "Of course."

"Do you want to go in the bed, or use the birthing stool?" Sherry was already helping her back out of the coat.

Tabitha's thoughts were more articulate than her speech allowed her to express. She thought back to the research paper she had completed on birthing traditions. "Stool...please... Gravity, right?"

"Right."

Back they went to the chair. Alex stayed with her while Sherry moved the coffee table back and spread a large plastic sheet on the living room floor. She thumped quickly up to her car, and returned with what looked like a wooden toilet seat on four short little legs.

"This is not very comfortable after a while, so I highly recommend that you walk around every ten minutes or so." Sherry looked Tabitha in the eyes. "You don't want a sore tailbone on top of everything else."

"Hello? Am I on time? Did I miss anything?" Aidie was at the door.

Tabitha let a fresh tide of pain carry her for an indeterminate time, squatting on the stool, while Alex rubbed her back and the midwives conferred quietly behind her.

When she opened her eyes again, Sherry was kneeling beside her and holding a glass with a straw.

"This is water mixed with corn syrup," she explained, offering the straw to Tabitha. "It's basically glucose, the same thing they'd give you in the hospital. I know you don't like needles, but you need to stay hydrated. As long as you keep sipping this, you won't need an intravenous."

Obediently, Tabitha sucked down a mouthful of glucose. "Ow! Ow, why are you doing that? Sherry, can you...tell her...not to do that?"

By her feet, Aidie had pressed the business end of her stethoscope to Tabitha's naked belly.

"Aidie has to listen to the baby's heartbeat." Sherry squeezed Tabitha's hand. "She has to do that between each contraction. We're with you, Tabitha. Let us know if you need us to break the membrane."

"How...how..." Tabitha felt mildly frustrated that her brain couldn't make her mouth move normally. "What...does...that...take?"

Sherry held up a long, slim stick, rather resembling a crochet hook. "All I do is put this in the right spot, and poke a little hole. It's like popping a balloon. I'd have to do it between contractions, but it shouldn't hurt, and it won't hurt the baby."

Tabitha nodded. "I'll let you know."

Time passed.

Tabitha concentrated on breathing. Her candles weren't lit, and her music wasn't playing, but those plans faded into the background as her body took charge. She was no longer in any kind of control. The labour was happening, and she was simply along for the ride.

After a while, she recalled her visualization techniques. As Alex, Sherry, and Aidie offered encouraging words and discussed her progress with quiet confidence, Tabitha tried to recall an image of peace and relaxation.

Finally, she had one.

The pains didn't seem to end. They simply overlapped. Words like "'crushing'" and "'crunching'" arose in her thoughts, though her body didn't feel ripped apart or torn in agony.

She focused on a beach she had once visited. With her eyes closed, she remembered standing in the cool water just at the edge of shore. How the grains of sand had felt between her toes and under the arch of her foot. The way the lapping waves had tickled the skin on her calves.

121

"Ow!" Aidie was back with her stethoscope. "Sherry, can you tell her to stop, please?"

"It's okay, honey," Alex whispered, kissing her cheek. "You're doing so well."

The unseen grip on her body tightened. Grunting, Tabitha leaned forward, her body drawing in on itself.

Her sweaty hand slipped on the wooden stool.

Alex was there to catch her.

"Lean on me, honey," he told her breathlessly. "You're great, you're doing great."

The moment ended, and Tabitha tried to sit up. Alex cradled her with his body. Her head rested against his shoulder.

She imagined the beach again. There was a small white shell by her right pinky toe. The sun was warm on her naked shoulders. A slight breeze moved the hair off her neck.

"Oooommph." The crushing, crunching pain was back. Obedient to its will, Tabitha bent forward again.

"Yes, that's it. Noise is good." Sherry patted her wrist. "Do you need me to break the water?"

"Noooo..." Tabitha shook her head. Sweat dripped down her temples, nose, and chin, pattering on the plastic sheet. "I'm...o...k..." She gritted her teeth.

"I really think you should get up and walk around."

Fixing Sherry with a steely gaze, Tabitha ground out her response. "Leave me alone."

Tabitha lost track of time.

She heard the rabbit thump in her cage, forgotten by all.

She heard the phone ring, and felt the floor shake as Aidie rose to bring the handset to Alex.

The quiet words were unimportant.

Tabitha invoked the image of the beach. The warm water tickling her skin. The tiny white spiral seashell drifting closer to her toes, carried on the tide.

Crush. Crunch.

"Okay," she whispered, whimpering. "Break the water."

Sherry moved swiftly to place a bowl under the stool. When Tabitha breathed again, she slid the thin instrument inside Tabitha's body and gave a little tug.

A gush of fluid poured neatly into the bowl. For a fleeting second, Tabitha felt some relief.

"Wow," Aidie remarked, "That was really tidy. Sometimes it splashes all over."

Crush. Crunch.

"Oooomph." Tabitha bent forward.

This time, the baby moved, too.

She felt the three individuals close in around her.

The pulsing, white-hot ache in her belly escalated, and then, impossibly, was nearly eclipsed by a fresh burning pain between her legs.

"The baby's crowning," Sherry told her calmly. "Push!"

Keening wildly, Tabitha bore down until she was out of breath.

Alex was by her shoulder. "You can do it, honey!"

Crush. Crunch.

Burning ring of fire.

Tabitha's head shook uncontrollably as she sat back from the second big push. She could hear herself sobbing.

Crush. Crunch.

Burning.

"There's the head!"

Tabitha cried out, her body arching backward. "Get it out! Get it out! Get it out!"

"Hold on, we have to clear the breathing passages." Beyond the burning pain, Tabitha sensed movement, but she had to fight to follow the next instruction. "Don't push yet."

"GET IT OUT!"

"Okay, now!"

With a mighty heave, Tabitha delivered her baby.

As her body came back down, and the infant emerged completely and neatly into Sherry's waiting, gloved hands, Tabitha was aware of only three things in her world: The incredible heat of her son's body as it passed between her thighs, the cessation of the pain, and the fact that she did, indeed, have a son. His manhood was clearly displayed under the umbilical cord, the testes round and swollen like pink mushrooms.

"It's a boy!" she cried triumphantly. Tabitha rested against Alex's shoulder while Sherry carefully turned the baby and placed him on Tabitha's now relaxed belly.

Just behind her, she heard Alex laughing with delight.

Tabitha wanted to hold him, but waited while Aidie wiped his back and arms, and Sherry clamped the cord.

"Do you want to...?" She offered the sanitized surgical scissors to Alex.

Tabitha felt him shake his head. "No, she needs me."

Love for her husband and their child filled her heart to bursting.

She barely noticed while Sherry carefully severed the connection between Tabitha and her baby. Lying on the cradle of her body, the infant did not cry. He simply looked up at her with the clearest blue eyes Tabitha had ever seen.

"Hello, little one," she said.

A straw appeared by her mouth. Tabitha took a sip.

"Now, you need to push one more time." Sherry caught Tabitha's attention. "Or try coughing. This shouldn't hurt."

Tabitha coughed. The placenta slid out as neatly as the rest. Sherry held it up for inspection.

"Isn't that remarkable?" Aidie's voice filled with awe. "This was your baby's home for nine months. It's a life support system. Nothing in science can match it."

"Tabitha, Alex, do you want to keep it?" Sherry asked. "We can put it in a bag and store it in your freezer. Some mothers like to bury them under trees."

"Yes, please." Tabitha only had eyes for her son. He had the same dimpled chin as his father. She traced one of his delicate ears with a trembling finger. It reminded her of a rose in full bloom. "One day, we'll have a yard, with a tree. I can keep it until then."

The baby blinked and yawned.

Tabitha turned her head toward her husband, who was still supporting her with his body. Alex met her lips with a firm, simple kiss.

"You did it, honey." He smiled at her.

"I love you."

"I love you, too."

The End

124

About the Author

Tori L. Ridgewood is a collector and teller of stories; a dedicated wife, mother, and high-school teacher; and is a practicing Wiccan. She enjoys reading, needlecraft, and overthinking movies.

toriridewood@hotmail.com

Other works by the author with Melange

Stories in Anthologies

Telltale Signs in Spellbound 2011
Mist and Midnight in Midnight Thirsts
A Living Specimen in Midnight Thirsts II

Learner Mum

by

Joanne Rawson

What a
Wonderful Pleasure
Meety you.
With love
Joanne Raw
☺ 13/2/2015

Learner Mum
Joanne Rawson

I love my life, my routine. There is absolutely nothing I would change, but then one weekend, I had a phone call that was about to change not only my sacred weekend but a part of me, too. For you to fully understand where I am coming from, let me tell you a little about myself, I promise it won't take long.

I come from a very religious background. Regardless of my parents preaching hell fire and brimstone, I have spent my entire life rebelling, unlike my younger sister, Wendy, the role model of morality, who has done it all by the big black book; courted, engaged, married and now raising a family. Although I am a successful freelance journalist slash writer, when I introduced Steve to my parents, straight away they knew he was the ideal husband for their then, twenty five year old daughter. Finally, I had found a man who could add stability to my life of debauchery. Steve is a morning presenter on one of Nottingham's local radio stations, and the only son of Clive Rutherford, MD and Susan Rutherford, a respected Pediatrician.

However, Steve and I have been living in what my parents call 'sin,' for the past eight years, we are so happy with our life, but to their disappointment, there are no signs of wedding bells or the patter of tiny feet on the horizon; Why?

Because, I hate babies, well perhaps hate is a little strong, and honestly speaking how can I hate something I don't know a bloody thing about? Don't misunderstand me, of course I'm fully aware of the biological know how, of how one gets a baby, trust me I've had my fair share of the practical, but NEVER, NEVER, have I been tempted in the least to follow the experiment through. I personally think all men's willies should be tattooed with a baby warning, like the stickers you see about dogs and Christmas in the back of a car window. It should read. A kid is for life, not for one night of sex.

And another thing, what is all this crap about my biological clock is ticking, or we just knew we were ready to start a family? So what do these people do? One night they are sitting watching their nightly soaps and the wife says instead of, "shall I defrost a chicken for dinner tomorrow?" she says, "I think we should start a family." Then the husband considers for a moment, during an advert and replies, "O.K. love, but after I've watched the news."

So now, you know that I, Polly Wilkins, am not in the least bit maternal.

* * * *

I stretched out in bed, rolled over onto my side and smiled at the bundle under the duvet.

Sheer bliss; it was Saturday, my favourite day of the week. Starting with passionate thoughts of a morning in bed with Steve, followed by a lazy lunch at the chic French bistro down the road, dunking string fries into our hot garlicky buttered mussels, while reading the tabloids. On the way home we'll walk along the river, stopping into the Greek supermarket to buy wine, cheese and bread, then spending a leisurely evening, chopping, marinating and sautéing our dinner while drinking wine, listening to music and talking about our week ahead.

Slithering up to Steve, I eased my body into the contours of his, running my hands around his thick fuzz of tummy hair. "Morning lover, its Saturday," I purred as I slid my hand around the elastic of his boxer shorts. Swiftly he rolled over on top of me, my hands rested on his shoulders, feeling the firmness of his muscles, reveling in how vibrant Steve could be first thing in a morning.

"God, I love Saturday's sex, and playing golf, I think I might have died and gone to heaven."

128

As he began to burrow his head into my neck, I pushed Steve away from me. "Sorry, golf?"

Steve let out a sign of exasperation. "I told you sweetie, Sam has the morning off. Promise I'll make it up to you."

Dropping his head, his tongue swirled around my breasts. Sliding under the duvet, he began doing his thing that made my whole body sing. I gave a moan of pleasure. Crawling back up, his head poked out of the duvet. 'So, it's ok then?"

"Oh, yes." I pushed him back under, and forgot about everything.

* * * *

I rolled over gasping for breath. Reaching out my arm, I grabbed my mobile, seeing WENDY on the screen of my phone. "This better be bloody important, to interrupt my Saturday morning sex."

I knew that this would make my prissy sister cringe on the other end of the phone, well, why wouldn't it? This was a woman who referred to sex, as "relations."

"I'll come straight to the point then," said Wendy.

"Funny, that's just what Steve was about to say!" I gave a smutty laugh down the phone, knowing that her face would now be pulsating with embarrassment, and her heart rate elevated at the mere thought of people copulating at this hour of the day.

"Yes, well, that's hardly something one should share. Polly, I need you to listen. Brian has this two day conference in Dublin. Normally, I stay at home, but this time partners have to attend. There is this gala dinner where Brian will get at least one award, and the Dublin CEO wants to meet us both. There is a big promotion coming up over there....."

I was becoming agitated at how long my sister was taking. "Stop," I interrupted. "Is this going to be a long conversation? If it is then I need to know, because my carnal desires are going off the boil here, Wendy."

"You can be so crass, Polly. Mum is laid up with her back. Dad can't get coverage at work. Polly, I need you to watch Josh."

For a moment, I was speechless, and then I broke out into hysterical laughter. "Sorry, Wendy, for one minute I thought you asked me to watch Josh."

"I did."

Steve was being annoying, trying to grab the phone from me. I pushed him away, guessing the look on my face said I was now in no mood. I said with anxiety, "Either this is a joke or Wendy is drunk, but she has just asked me to look after Josh for two days."

Steve rolled back onto his side of the bed, cracking up with laughter. Through the laughing I could just make out, "She must be drunk."

"Wendy, are you ok? Is this some kind of after birth depression?"

Wendy gave a heavy sigh. "I think you mean post natal depression, and no I went through that after Josh was born. He's nearly a year old."

"Really, he's one? Is this why you are depressed? Because, I always thought he was a little slow."

"Polly," Wendy screamed at me over the phone line, "Josh is average for his age. Now will you blinking well help me out or not?"

I sat bolt upright in bed. I could feel my heart beating faster, the tightness in my chest constricting my every breath. I was the last person my sister would ask to look after her first born. Hell, Wendy knew that I couldn't even look after their goldfish for a week without killing them. How the hell could I keep a baby alive?

Now hyperventilating, Steve took control, as Steve always did when it came to my family.

Assuring Wendy, Steve told her everything would be fine. Steve had learned the art of pacifying the Wilkins family down to a tea. It was amazing how just the calmness of his voice, and the serenity on his face, could get them to agree to anything when it came to me.

As he put the phone down, a wave of hysteria took over me, and I screamed, "What the hell were you thinking? Neither of us have any idea about bloody babies?' Feeling a churning in my tummy, I ran to the bathroom to puke.

* * * *

Later that morning, I stood like a limpet in our lounge, Steve holding Josh while he listened to Wendy read through the list of do's and don'ts. I watched in horror as my brother in law, carried in bags, buggies, boxes of toys, books and more food than I could possibly imagine a small person could consume in two days. Were my eyes deceiving me, or was the last load a bundle of nappies? Finally, the list of contact numbers, the hotel, doctor, and health visitor. The list seemed endless! Bloody hell, this child had more of an entourage than a ruddy rock star.

Finally, after a lot a kissing and hugging, and my sister leaving in floods of tears, well, I'm not surprised I wouldn't leave my only child with me and Steve left holding the baby. Literally.

Naturally, I assumed Steve would forgo his weekly worship of Golf. How very naïve of me to think that, after all, he was a faithful disciple of the game. Like Mecca calling them to the hallowed clubhouse, even a baby could not outplay golf.

Steve had played it very sly, keeping Josh amused, leading me into a false sense of security. Though, my sister had asked me to babysit my nephew, Steve would be the actual one making all the baby decisions, or so I thought.

I had spent the first hour of Josh's arrival trying to look busy, so I actually did not have to look after him. Whereas, Steve was a natural, which seemed strange seeing as he was an only child with no other siblings in his family near his age. I on the other had had been five when Wendy had been born. While my friends played mummies and daddies, I played 'A Team' and knight rider with the boys from our neighbourhood. Sneaking up behind me, Steve slipped his hands under my t-shirt, cupping my small breasts in his hands, while he nuzzled my neck. "So, here is a little taster, for when I get home, and that little chappie is in bed."

I spun around. Please don't tell me you are still going to play golf?"

"Sweetie, I told you, and you did agree."

"Yes, but that was when you had your head between my legs and before Wendy called. No, Steve, I can't let you leave me alone with Josh."

We then had one of those strange fights that are conducted in a whisper, where hand gestures are emphasized, just so we would not upset the baby. Steve tried to get around me with false promises of bubble baths, wine and Johnson's baby oil when he got home, to which I pointed to my nephew, who sat chuckling in his play pen, obviously thinking that auntie and uncle were putting on some kind of skit for his benefit.

"Really, Steve, if you think leaving me here, on my own, sex is going to happen tonight, think again."

Steve took me in his arms, kissed me and turned my head to Josh. "Look at him. What can possibly go wrong? He's a little angel. Trust me, Polly, you will be fine." With that she heard a car horn outside. "That will be Sam. Love you." Steve left waving to Josh, leaving me standing, helpless.

It had been a nightmare. No sooner had Steve left, Josh who had been quite happy sitting in his playpen, gurgling and laughing while Steve played peek a boo, began howling. I had taken note; I'm not completely stupid. Steve had made him laugh with a green frog. Picking it up I began trying to imitate the same frog noises that I had heard Steve make, however, mine sounded more like a frog belching, not croaking, and Josh didn't seem to find it funny at all, in fact he howled even louder.

"Ok, Ok, how about the…" Pulling the string bag of toys to me I delved in. The felt bell thing. Listen Josh, listen to the bell." I rattled it vigorously.

Josh now had a blotchy tearstained face that was becoming redder by the minute. I tried every toy in the bag, but nothing pacified him. Exasperated, I had no idea what to do next; walking around the lounge, covering my ears from the noise, what did this child have for lungs, bellows? Jean downstairs must have thought the same thing as she banged on the ceiling of her flat. Normally, this only happened late at night when Steve and I played our music too loud.

"You see, this is exactly why little people scare the hell out of me. How am I supposed to know what he wants?"

Turning around I looked at Josh. He now had his arms outstretched. Timidly, I bent down to pick him up, trying to recall if I'd ever held him before, wondering if I held him too tight, would he burst, or if he struggled to free himself, could I drop him on the floor? However, Josh seemed to know the protocol, wrapping his chubby little arms around my neck, his little legs automatically seemed to cling around my waist. Suddenly the howling stopped, just a slight sobbing. As he sucked his thumb the sobs stopped and he placed his head in the crook of my neck.

I began to walk around the lounge, stepping over the mass of discarded toys. I don't know why I began softly shushing, it just seemed the logical thing to do. Surprisingly, I felt my nephew beginning to relax, so much so, that within a few minutes he had fallen asleep. For another fifteen minutes, I walked around the flat, shushing, not daring to put him down, in case he woke up again, I don't know about Josh being exhausted from all that crying, but it had tired the hell out of me. I felt physically drained. How did Wendy do this every day? Eventually the weight of Josh was bearing a strain on my back, so with great care, and bated breath, I lowered him into his travel cot that Brian had put up in our bedroom, (how thoughtful!) then I collapsed on our bed, and prayed that Steve would be home before Josh woke up.

* * * *

After an hour, my head had cleared. Tiptoeing to the kitchen, I was in need of a drink. Forcing all my self-control not to pour myself a large glass of chardonnay, I opted for an herb tea. Waiting for the kettle to boil, I picked up Wendy's lists of notes, lists being the operative word since it was like a bloody epic. I had written short stories that had less of a word count than this. It seemed, as I skipped through the list, that a whimpering cry means he just needs picking up. The uncomfortable cry, he needs changing. The hungry cry, the I need sleep cry. What the heck was all that about? Surely, a cry is a cry?

Then the time table; I thought Josh was a human being but it seemed Wendy had a robot. Breakfast at seven, lunch at one, I glanced at my watch, it was gone three, never mind it said tea at four, I'll just double up, trying not to see the capital letters at the bottom, saying 'PLEASE STICK TO THE ROUTINE.' I was contemplating the don't let him sleep too long in the afternoon when the doorbell gave out its shrill ring, followed by some persistent knocking.

As I ran to answer the door, cursing the person on the other side, I was sure I heard Josh cry. Opening the door, there stood Marjorie my Avon lady, in her brassy voice shouting, "Avon calling.

"Shush, he's asleep." I motioned to the open bedroom door.

"Sorry, love, I thought Sexy Steve would be at the match? So he's here then?" She strained her double chin and saggy neck to see into the flat. Marjorie, in her mid-forties but looked a tired fifty something, would have passed more as an old fishwife not a representative of cosmetics. Poor thing had a massive crush on Steve, and when she realised that he was the voice on the radio she swooned over every morning, the poor cow became a gibbering wreck around Steve, laughing and fluttering her over made up eyes, and pouting her cerise pink lips, I don't know who I am more embarrassed for, her or Steve.

"It's my nephew, actually. The first time I've ever had him," I whispered.

"Got a bit of the jitters have you? Well you'll be fine, it comes natural to women, the maternal instinct. Bet by the end of today you will be begging Steve for one of your own."

"I doubt it. I'm not cut out at for this mother malarkey, and all that pushing and shoving." I shivered at the thought. Right on cue, Josh began whimpering from the bedroom.

"Sounds like a hungry cry to me."

"You know what that cry means?" This was amazing. Did women have a seventh sense transplanted in them when they gave birth?

"Should do, love, I've had five. After the second one it's like shelling peas. On the last one I said to the young whipper-snapper of a midwife not much older than my eldest, *it's coming.* She said not yet, Mrs. Glover, I said you'd better get down there and catch the little bugger. Before she could say push, out she flew." Josh gave another cry. Marjorie tilted her head like a wise old owl. "Yes, sounds like he wants feeding. I'll let you get on. I'll call back in the week, bye love."

I was sorely tempted to ask Marjorie to stay, five children, well, she must be an expert, but she was already tottering down the corridor.

Closing the door, wanting to kick myself, I should have lured her in on a pretence Steve would be back shortly. Or why hadn't I just admitted I needed help, that this whole situation was well and truly out of my depth, and what was it Marjorie had said? It comes natural to women, the maternal instinct. As far back as I could remember, I'd never had a maternal instinct in my life. Perhaps I was a freak. Suddenly I pictured myself as a sideshow freak, at Nottingham Goose Fair. Steve in his candy stripe waistcoat and straw boater shouting, "Roll up, roll up, see the woman with no maternal instincts.' People pointing fingers at me disgusted, shaking their head in shame.

As I walked into the bedroom, feeling sorry for Steve having only half a woman, Josh gave me a big grin, whereupon something weird happened to me, for one second, just one second mind, I was sure my heart turned to putty.

Taking Josh from his cot, I softly said, "Come on you, let's have something to eat." I brushed his curly blonde hair back off his face, at which point, my nephew wrapped his arms around my neck and placed an open wet slobbery kiss on my cheek. "Now then, don't get all soppy on me." I choked back a tear, catching a glimpse of myself in the mirror, I had to admit, perhaps it did suit me. Oh no, don't think I'm getting all mushy, my clock's ticking and all that crap. It all soon changed.

The reins on the high chair seemed to be an exercise from the Krypton Factor. It seemed common sense that they would fit like a parachute harness, not that I'd ever been parachuting, but I was beginning to feel like I was about to be pushed out of a plane without a parachute.

Both Josh and I began to sweat as I tried this way and that trying to bend his little arms. Eventually, with more luck than judgment, Josh was safely strapped in.

Josh obviously knew there was some gastronomic delight about to appear in front of him as he excitedly banged on his tray with his plastic spoon, while I read my feeding instructions. Hearing the ting, of the microwave, I took out the contents and tipped it into the bowl. "Yea god's what is this?" It smelt like mashed potatoes and veg, with gravy, but looked like something a dog had thrown up. Placing it in front of Josh, he seemed to think it looked appetising. "Bonne appetite, and for dessert, yummy strained apples." I grimaced.

Thinking now Josh would be happy, he had food, I would grab myself a sandwich. I was about to turn around to the fridge, when the bowl came hurtling over in my direction, splattering all down the front of my t-shirt. Salvaging what I could that was still in the bowl, I placed it back down in front of him, only to have a repeat performance, and Josh chuckling, thinking he was very funny.

"No, this is not funny. Here." I shoveled a mouthful of slop into his mouth and, hungry for more, he opened his mouth again. I pulled up a chair, and sat in front of Josh and asked, "You like this?" From nowhere, my voice became soft, and gentle, as I smiled at my nephew. "Open wide. Here comes another. I think I'm getting better at this, don't you?" I spoke too soon, as Josh picked up the bowl, and promptly deposited it on my head.

* * * *

This was not me. I am Polly Wilkins, the independent career women, a free spirit, who never lets anything, get the better of her. Yet, it still did not stop the tears and mashed potato falling in globs from my chin, as I pulled congealed dinner out of my hair. All I wanted to do was lock the bathroom door, draw a hot bubble bath, and try to forget about today, in the hope that when I emerged fresh and revived, I would find Steve, starting to prepare dinner and it had all been a very bad dream. But I couldn't. I'd left Josh, much as myself, covered in food, yet as happy as a pig in muck, grinding a rusk into the remains of his dinner on his tray. Shoving my head under the shower, I quickly rinsed my hair, grabbed a towel, and wrapped it around my head.

* * * *

As I walked down the hallway, it hit me like a smack in the chops. "Oh my God what is that smell?" Had old Mr Thompson's cat sneaked into the flat again? Or worse, Mr Thompson himself, both renowned for roaming the corridors, and wandering into any flat where they found the door unlocked. I'm not saying Mr T, like his cat, left a steaming package in a corner, or peed up a chair leg, let's just say a quick hello to Mr T left your eyes stinging from the pungent ammonia pong. Only last month, I had padded naked out of the shower to find Mr T sitting on the sofa watching another grueling rerun of Murder She Wrote. Needless to say, that social call not only cost us an arm and a leg in steam cleaning, but now trying to avoid Mr T, who, when he looked at me, obviously only saw me naked.

Wandering around the lounge, I could not find any cat poop, and the smell definitely was not as strong in here, I retraced my steps back to the hall, it seemed to be coming from the kitchen. Strangely, as I got nearer to Josh, the smell got increasingly worse. I didn't need to be Einstein to know, seeing the strain on Josh's face, what was happening down there in the depths of his nappy.

I looked up to the heavens above, hoping that someone up there would know what to do in this moment of sheer need. "Please, if you really have any feelings for my weak stomach, Steve will walk through that door right now."

I looked at the door, willing it to open. I had to think fast on my feet, after all, wasn't that what mothers did in emergency situations like these? They would spin around, and turn into Wonder Mum, or in my case, Blunder Woman. Whatever. I had to get Josh out of his cackey nappy, if not only for my sake, this was surely a hazard to the environment. It was then I spied my rubber gloves. "Good, now those will come in useful, it's bound to be messy down there." Just thinking about it made my tummy churn, and then like resolving a mathematical equation, I pulled open a kitchen drawer and rifling through, I found what I was looking for, a surgical mask. Steve had bought each of us one for our trip to Asia, when the scares were on about bird flu. Togged up in my rubber gloves and mask, I took Josh to the changing mat, holding him way out at arm's length. Josh had a worried look on his face, not quite making out what was happening, and why his strange aunt seemed to resemble the masked person who brought him out into the world.

Perhaps he thought I was about to push him back. Believe me, if Wendy walked into the room now, I would.

Things were going fine. Josh seemed happy to lie there, as I took off his trousers, then peeling back the little plastic tabs, and opening up his nappy, I took one whiff, and instantly began to wretch. "This is definitely not what I have just fed you. Dear god in heaven, what does my sister feed this child, fertiliser?" I began to pull the nappy away from Josh. "Yuck, yuck, yuck," I whined, trying not to look, but at the same time, trying to roll the nappy, but the sticky tabs just would not stick. The last thing I wanted was it to unfold and. "Oh! I can't bear to think what is inside." Grabbing Steve's golfing magazine, I wrapped the nappy inside. "There, that will teach him to leave me." And then it happened, something that I was not expecting, a fountain of pee, shot into the air. Jeeze, could this day get any worse? Josh, with a load off his mind, and visibly enjoying his freedom, his little legs kicking in glee—well let's face it, how would you like to walk around all day with a cowpat stuck to your bum.

Through the gagging and the heaving, I managed to clean his bum, when the telephone rang. "You just stay there," I instructed Josh, keeping one hand firmly on his tummy, as I reached for the phone.

"Hi, it's me," my sister said. By the sounds of her happy, slightly slurred voice, she'd had a pre-dinner sherry. "Just thought I would call and see how things are going."

"Oh, it's all tickety-boo here." My response sounded more sarcastic than I'd planned, but hopefully Wendy's one sherry had numbed her perception.

"Sorry, Polly, this is a really bad line, you sound muffled, perhaps its being overseas."

Yes the Croft's Original, had kicked in. I had forgotten the furthest Wendy had dared venture on her travels was Jersey, and then she had worried about drinking the water, and if the food would be different, after all Jersey had French connections. Fighting to take my mask off, in the process my towel fell over my face. Feeling my hair, it now felt like cardboard, from not washing all of the food out.

"So I thought I would just say goodnight to my little munchkin."

My heart skipped a beat as I looked around frantically. Josh had disappeared off his changing mat. "He's not here, because..." *Come on, think, Polly think, what would Wonder Mum say?* I had now jumped up searching for my nephew under cushion covers, behind the sofa, "...because, he's already asleep. You know, after a full day playing with his aunt Polly, the little darling is knackered."

"Oh, bless his little cotton sock. So give him a big kiss from me when you see him."

"Oh, I certainly will. Bye," I said and abruptly ended the phone call.

I scanned the room for the little fellow—well—he could hardly have gone far, but in the next few minutes far enough to make my lounge look like a war zone. There was a mighty crash, and the tower of CDS fell to the floor, followed by a chortle, I dashed over to find Josh, crawling over Steve's pride collection, making his way towards my bookcase. Before I had a chance, he began pulling out my cherished books, only to see him pick up my treasured copy of Little Women, and began sucking the cover, and in all the excitement, and nappyless, I could not help and smile as Josh peed on Steve's autographed copy of Tony Jacklin's autobiography.

* * * *

This had been the hardest day's work I had done in my life. The next time an editor rings me up gnashing their teeth down the phone, wanting the article yesterday, I would hold my artistic temperament back and think of today. No amount of verbal abuse and threatening to sack me, because I was inadequate, could possibly be as daunting as today, and it was by no stretch of the imagination over yet. I did not have a clue where to start. Josh needed to be cleaned up, from his dinner/ tea, the lounge needed blitzing, the kitchen, well, I wasn't even going to think about the mess *that* was in, and I hadn't even begun to consider what I was doing for dinner.

I collapsed on the sofa, in need of adult stimulation. Switching on the television, a tacky game show was about to begin. As the music started, Josh tossed aside my now desecrated book, and crawled towards the telly. He began clapping along to the cheesy music. I had to laugh, or I just knew if I didn't I would break down and cry from exhaustion. When the music ended, Josh became bored. He crawled towards me, grabbing a plastic book on the way in his chubby fingers. Placing it on my knee, he pulled himself up.

With a heavy sigh, I picked him up and sat him at the side of me. "What do we have here?" I flicked the book over and read "my first book of letters. A is for apple...." Josh wriggled until he was sitting on my knee.

* * * *

Steve's key turned in the lock. As he walked through the door, he gave his usual greeting, "Hi honey, I'm home." This normally put a smile on my face, but as I heard that familiar comforting voice, that until today I took for granted, an effervescence of mixed emotions bubbled through my entire being.

"Polly, we didn't stop at the pub. Sam said we should have a beer at…bloody hell, Polly, what's happened?"

Steve looked around the living room; no doubt, thinking we had been robbed, or even worse a siege had taken place at 27A Sherwood House, then noticing me, sitting in a helpless state on the sofa. My soft curly blonde hair had dried stiff, which had formed tiny globules of mash, resembling a very bad case of dandruff, and a stiff Gucci t-shirt that looked like I'd been wearing it for weeks. Steve had come home to find the female version of Mr Thompson.

My emotions took over and through a mouthful of blubbering, I said, "Oh, Steve, I'm sorry, I did my best, but there was all the crying, the throwing of food, crappy nappies…" I gasped for air, "Oh and Steve, Josh peed on Tony Jacklin."

Steve sat beside me on the sofa, taking me into his arms. "Shush, shush, it's alright, I'm here now, I'm so sorry baby."

Sam was accustomed to female hormonal outbursts having been happily married to Jackie for eight years, with a six-year-old son, and a daughter, age three, bent down and scooped Josh up from the floor, like a rugby ball. "Hey there little chap, what have you been doing to your aunt Polly?"

I couldn't bring myself to look at Sam; I could not bear to see the triumph on his face, that after teasing me many times when we'd all spent evenings together, he would always say in a drunken stupor. "Polly I love you. You've a killer rack, the best arse I've ever seen, but you would be a crap mum." With that we would all burst out laughing.

I saw his hand rest on Steve's arm, softly and with concern, he said, "Steve, mate, Polly's been great looking after Josh, I think you should get her into a nice warm bath while I take care of Josh."

With that, Steve put his arms around my waist, lifted me from the sofa, and guided me like an invalid towards the bathroom, I stopped for a second, and gave Sam a grateful smile.

* * * *

Steve had undressed me, while he drew the bath, and then helped me in. Sitting on the toilet, he said, "Really, Polly, you did so well today. I am so proud of you. To tell you the truth, I was having second thoughts. Looking after a baby that is not your own is a massive responsibility and so scary, especially if you do something wrong. Perhaps you would feel different if it was your own?"

My body tensed. 'What do you mean it would be different with my own?"

"I meant, in general. Any person who had never looked after a baby would feel as you did, but once they had their own, it would all work out."

"Work out, Steve? Work out? You make it sound like doing a crossword. Have you any idea what I went through today? I, me, Polly, was not in control. I'm always in control, but today I didn't know what to do." I gave a small sob. "Perhaps Marjorie was right."

Steve looked bemused. "Marjorie, the Avon lady? What does she have to do with it?"

I lay back in the bath, sloshing water over my body. I knew I had spoken without thinking. What if Steve thought I was right? I was not all women. Would I lose him? Then I had the most dreadful thought; what if I was only half a woman? Did this mean I was a closet lesbian?

"I am so, so sorry, you are living with only half a woman."

By the end of my tale, and after expressing my fears, Steve raised himself off the toilet, leaned forward, and kissed me on the nose. "You are far from a showground freak. You are sexy, sensationally seductive, and talented. Perhaps your need for independence makes you a little highly strung on certain issues, but I love you, Polly, I always have and always will. Now relax and I'll get Josh ready for bed, and then start dinner." He stood up, went towards the door, stopping for a moment he turned. "I suppose we could always try the closet lesbian thing out... I've always wondered what a threesome would be like, only in the call of duty to check your theory out. What about that redhead in the newsroom at the station, do you fancy her?"

I threw a soaking wet sponge at Steve. "Get out, you perv!" I laughed.

* * * *

As I lay back in the bath, I could hear the mumbles of Steve and

Sam, followed by a filthy laugh; obviously, Steve had enlightened Sam about the closet lesbian fear, and his idea of how to test it out. I know Steve would not divulge the part about having second thoughts, and the whole scary issue of looking after someone else's baby, it wasn't a thing men did, bearing all to each other, no matter how good friends they were. This had all been explained to me a few months after Steve had moved in. I ran some more hot water, smiling to myself as I soaped my sponge. I may be a complete moron, at looking after babies, but there was one thing I was good at, writing, and unbeknown to Steve and Sam, they had just given me a great idea for next month's column. "Are all men afraid to talk?"

Steve had been horrified when I told him that my friend Janice was having problems in the bedroom department with her boyfriend.

Midway to his mouth, his French fry dangled, dripping with garlic butter. "Why? Why would you talk about something so personal, Polly, why?"

"Come on, Steve, don't tell me you and your friends don't swap notes about women. Just think of it as free therapy."

I could see his brain going faster than the speed of light, as to what I may have told them, and I knew exactly what he would ask next. It was just a matter of time; three, two, one, his eyebrow raised, here it came.

"Do you talk about us...? You know if I'm good, bad or in different?"

I wasn't about to mushroom his male ego, that my friends already envied my man, and tell him they called him Marathon Man, on account of his stamina to perform at least twice a night, now that would just make his head explode.

Nonchalantly, I stabbed a mussel and sucked it off my fork, allowing the garlic butter to trickle down my throat. "So you and Sam, never talk, you never ask for advice, say when I asked you to move in?"

"Not really, it's a man thing. He would have thought I was a right wuss. So tell me, do you talk about technique and stamina?"

A tap came on the bathroom door. "Polly." It was Sam. "That was Jackie on the phone, she will call you later."

"Thanks, Sam." I slid under the water. Just great, a nurturing call from Jackie, just what I didn't need; Nottingham's answer to a Stepford wife.

* * * *

When I appeared from my wonderful soak in the bath, hair soft and gleaming and smelling of my favourite perfume, Coco Chanel, I found that Sam had already left. Jackie had called again. They were just on their way out to dinner, and called to say we should go over for Sunday lunch tomorrow. JOY!

Steve, bless his cotton socks, had dinner almost ready and the table set, candles lit, crystal glasses at the ready and a bottle of Marques de Grinon, my favourite Rioja, opened and ready to pour. He kissed me and sat me at the table, flicked my napkin and slid it onto my knee like a true headwaiter. Pouring me a glass of wine, he said dinner would be ready in five minutes. I felt so relaxed and ready for this wonderful pampering I was about to receive, when I suddenly realised that something was missing. "OMG! Where is Josh?" I had completely forgotten about him.

"Don't panic, Polly. Josh is out to the world. Sam bathed him, I fed him and got him into his Jim Jams. God love him, he's fast asleep in the travel cot at the side of our bed. So you relax and enjoy dinner, ok?"

I don't believe it. I had just experienced the most traumatic day of my life trying to be mother to the little tiger and failing dismally and along came Steve, who has everything under control in less than thirty minutes. I felt a total failure.

* * * *

Next day we pulled up outside Jackie and Sam's; much like them, their home was a pretentious, four storey Victorian mansion, complete with gravel drive, and a line of conifers, along with Sam's BMW and Jackie's 4x4 the driveway was full of cars I didn't recognise. It all became clear when we walked into the lounge to find it full of thirty plus something couples, sipping orange juice and cranberry juice while hoards of children rampaged around the place.

"Come in, come in," said Jackie in her Stepford Wife Capri pants, turtle neck jumper and pearls. "Everyone, this is Steve and Polly."

The room went silent, as couples turned to Steve and I. False smiles dropped as they eyed my faded ripped jeans, cropped jumper, and my good old faithful bikers boots I'd had forever. As I glanced around the room, all the women seemed to be dressed like my mother and sister; it seemed the dress code was British Home Stores, or Country Casuals.

"Great," I whispered through gritted teeth to Steve. "Smug married couples."

Steve smiled and acknowledged our existence. Gritting his teeth, he replied, "Just smile, and for the love of god, don't mention you don't want children."

I glared up at Steve, about to protest that I would not lie, when Jackie placed a glass of cranberry juice in my hand, and whisked Josh out of Steve's arms. "Polly, Steve, I just want the pair of you to relax, forget about Josh. Golly, there are enough nannies here to take care of him, mix and enjoy yourselves." She winked at Steve.

"Why did she do that?"

"What?"

"Wink at you."

"Polly, have you seen six-bellies Sam and his receding hairline? Look around, all the men in Aran and corduroy. If you were a suppressed housewife, wouldn't you wink at a hunk like me?" Steve joked. Anyway the hot chick in the tweed skirt and brogues has just offered me a nibble." Walking off in her direction, Steve stopped to take a cocktail sausage from the thirty year old Miss Marple, he muttered something in her ear, and then seductively popped the sausage in his mouth, leaving Miss Marple, flushed with ecstasy. Daringly, she opened the top button of her crisp white blouse.

"So I hear that you are looking after your nephew." I turned to see a very tall, heavy boned woman, dressed in cord jeans, creases down the front that could cut paper, a checked shirt, and cashmere sweater draped around her shoulders. "That is so now. My sister Cassandra had a budding career in finance, but when she got married her husband so wanted children, and she was so not thinking she could handle it. So I said, take one of mine for the weekend. I have three and do you know she so absolutely was meant to have children."

Before I could say I was just helping my sister out, not having my nephew as a test for the weekend to see if I liked motherhood or not, I was circled by two other women; Miss Marple, and a heavily pregnant woman who constantly rubbed her bump.

"But I thought Jackie said you weren't married?" inquired Miss Marple, still pink from what I assume was the first time she'd had even a flutter of an orgasm, after Steve and his chipolata joke. "Not that I am against having children out of wedlock, per say. Golly, I know heaps of people, my cleaning lady, my hairdresser's daughter, and I think—yes, my odd job man's granddaughter, but then what does one expect from the working class."

"Oh really, Pru, you are such a stick in the mud," said the bump rubber. "I'm sure Polly and Steve will get married first, however there's many a slip between cup and lip."

I liked this lady, although a bit too Lady Diana pre divorce for me, so I had to stop myself from saying, *if she meant a slip with lips and dick*, but I didn't think these women would quite see the funny side of my joke. I was in Wendy's world. God how she would be lapping it up. It seemed all I could hear was baby talk. This was hell on earth that only your married friends could inflict on you. No, I retract that. Sam was Steve's friend. I only tolerated Jackie, and these people were a load of knob heads. Did I really have to listen to this all afternoon? I leaned forward. "Actually..." Three excited faces expected to hear wedding bells announced, when I continued, "I have no intention of marrying Steve, and as for babies, well, my uterus has a no entry sign." With my head held high and my working class pride, I walked away, knowing I had achieved the result I was looking for, three up their own arses, gobsmacked women.

I headed off to the garden. It seemed the men were congregating out there, and hopefully would find a hip flask with some vodka for my cranberry juice.

I joined Steve and Sam talking to another man, feeling safe in male company, no talk of marriage, or sprogs.

"Ah, Polly," said Sam, gritting a Churchill cigar between his teeth. 'Meet Myles, he works for the Times, financial pages. Polly is freelance."

Myles was a weedy looking man with a face like a ferret. "May I have read your articles?"

'I doubt it—women's glossy'—that type of thing. I also do a monthly column in a weekend paper."

"And she's got three novels under her belt, racy stuff. Jackie won't let me read them, says it'll increase my libido." I flinched as Sam pinched my bum.

I could see the beads of perspiration appear on the ferret's forehead; he wiped the corners of his drooling mouth with a hanky. "Are you married Polly?"

Oh, god, here we go again. It was always the first question men asked when they knew about the books, imagining I wrote on experience, and that I was a real Little Miss Dynamite in bed. Didn't these imbeciles know that we writers had an imagination?

"No..." Not able to finish my sentence before old Ferret face came out with the usual one-liners, what's a great woman like you...that my partner was standing in our company.

Sam slapped his stomach, which rippled grotesquely under his Fred Perry. "She's one of *them*."

'Oh, you're a lesbian?' Ferret's eyes lit up like Roman Candles.

Sam laughed. "Not for the want of finding out, hey Polly?" Sam gave me a nudge, nudge, wink, wink say no more gesture. "No, our Polly here doesn't agree with marriage."

Steve could see the irritation in my face and feared my reactions as A: Sam would dare to inform a complete stranger of my fears, last night. B: Sam had committed sin number three in my list of commandments; do not interrupt me before I have finished. One being, don't ask me if I'm married. Two, just because I'm a woman, don't talk to me like I'm stupid.

A look of concern loomed on the ferret's face. "Oh, you should think about it, time ticking by, and a fine specimen like you, would rear a top pup. What a shame."

Steve now was noticeably worried, even more so when his phone rang, and he knew he had to leave me alone, fearing the worst. "Polly, it's your sister on the phone, would you like to take it?" The willingness in his voice, begged me to take the call.

"You take it. I just have to finish here."

I returned my gaze to ferret face; I am sure my eyes must have turned red as the blood pumped into my head.

Was that how men looked at women? As specimens? If we had a wet nose and stood well, that we could produce them a champion breed? How ironic they should be so big headed. From a woman's point of view, did they know the pickings on offer? Where has the man's man gone? The majority of the modern men are dorks, and that included most of them here this afternoon.

I was just about to lecture my learned males, when Steve grabbed my arm, almost dragging me across the grass. "Sorry, Sam, must dash. Wendy is waiting for us back at the flat."

Protesting, I hadn't quite finished, Steve manhandled me through the lounge, past the gawking faces of the Witches of Nottingham, still in shock from my no entry uterus, and into the car.

Steve revved up the car like a formula one driver. "Steve!"

"Don't talk to me. I already know about the uterus, and I could see you building up for Myles."

"Yes but, Steve," I protested, as we sped down the road.

"Polly, shut up. This 'no marriage and babies' issue is beginning to bore me. Have you ever considered my feelings?"

"Steve, I just wanted to say, we've forgotten Josh."

* * * *

With Josh, safe and sound and back with my sister, Steve and I sat in silence. I tried to concentrate on my book and Steve was trying to look interested in a nature program.

In the past, Steve had been so easy going about not getting married and having babies. When people asked he always shrugged the idea away, saying, "Why do we need to conform?" Just being together was enough to show how much we loved each other. So why the hell was he so dammed annoyed?

We had played the 'everything is fine game' with Wendy and Brian, chatting about Brian's new job offer, tongue in cheek how we had loved having Josh, (forgetting to mention driving off and leaving him) and laughed when Wendy suggested we might now tie the knot, and start our own little brood. Then as soon as they had left, Steve completely ignored me. When I questioned what should we cook for dinner, he plonked a take away menu under my nose, his order already written on a scrap of paper.

More to the point, why did I feel, so bad? As I thought about it, I should have known last night, this confrontation was coming. Over dinner, Steve suggested we should think about a bigger place. I had laughed it off, saying why would the two of us need somewhere bigger. When we went to bed that night, I walked into our bedroom to find Steve leaning with his head resting on his hand, staring into the cot, watching Josh sleep. "Just look how peaceful he looks. Doesn't it just make you want to pick him up?"

"Yes, if you want to spend all night playing Croaking Frog and reading My first Alphabet." My joke didn't trigger even a smile.

Then the next morning, Steve was already up and out when I awoke. He had left a note saying he and Josh had gone to get papers and have a walk down by the canal. When he came back, he showed me the pictures he had taken of Josh on his phone, feeding the ducks, having printed them off, the one of Josh laughing into the camera, was now propped up against the clock.

I began to wonder if at some point in our relationship, there would come a time when Miss Poppy Wilkins was not enough for Steve?

"Steve, are we o.k.?" I asked hastily. My voice had a slight quiver.

He turned his head slowly from the TV. He didn't say anything, but the way he looked at me, I had never felt so scared. "Steve you're scaring me here." I jumped from the sofa and knelt beside him. 'You're right, I am highly strung and don't consider your feelings, but for the last few hours I've thought about nothing else." I seized his hands and added, "Really thought. The reason I feel so strongly about marriage, is that nearly half of our friends were like us, so happy until they got married. Now look at them. Divorced, desperate and dejected. I don't want that to happen to us, Steve."

He turned off the TV and sat for a moment looking at a blank screen. I could feel the tears building up behind my eyes. "What about the others, Polly, the ones that are happy? Or is it the whole idea of committing yourself to one person, me perhaps?" His face had turned pale, that one only associated with fear, I had never seen him look like this. It was as if a stranger was sitting in front of me.

"No," I gasped. "I love you so much. I couldn't bear life without you. I'd be so lost."

For a moment he gazed into my eyes. I knew Steve could always tell what I was feeling by my eyes, I prayed he knew what I was feeling now. He drew his head closer to mine, cupped my cheeks in his hands, his lips slowly brushed mine.

"I love you, Polly, and I you know you love me. Why don't you just admit that standing in a church full of our family and friends, only scares you because you can't control the outcome. You can't write the ending. It scares me too, but I love you enough, and so damned sure that both of us would never let it fail, and you know why?" I shook my head; the tears, I couldn't hold back, flowed down my cheeks. "Because you are strong enough for the both of us to make it work. Show me how much you really love me, Polly." A tear slowly trickled down his cheek and he pulled me onto his knee. His lips covered mine; it was a long kiss, a desperate kiss, tasting of both our tears and passion for each other. Steve wrapped his arms around me, I could feel the strength of his body harden, and with no effort at all, rose from the chair and carried me to

147

the bedroom.

Steve ran his fingers through my long blonde hair, entwined it around his hand and leaning down he inhaled deeply. "I love the way your hair smells of Channel and coconut." Kissing my eyes, he said, "The first time I saw you I was blown away how your piercing blue eyes are like two deep pools. I just wanted to dive into them, and this nose, that twitches when you concentrate." He kissed its tip. Then with great tenderness, Steve began to undress me, kissing down my neck as he lifted my jumper over my head. "I love your long slender neck, and these breasts that you think are too small, I think are perfect." Cupping them in his hands, he placed a small kiss on each.

Throwing back my head, I gasped for air, every nerve ending stimulated by each caress, each kiss driving me into a state of euphoria. I ran my hands through his hair. "Take me, take me now," I groaned.

Taking my hand, he led me to the bed. Slipping under the crisp cool sheets I became aware of how hot my body felt, like a fire roaring under my skin. As Steve slid in beside me, our bodies entwined, Steve looked down at me, "Polly will you marry me?"

My eyes widened, I licked my lips tasting Steve, my heart thumped with excitement and fear. I slid my hands down the side of his face, pulling his quivering lips toward mine. I could feel his warm breath, waiting in anticipation for my answer. "Yes," I said. His mouth came onto mine with passionate hunger, and then our bodies became one.

As dawn was breaking, we lay on our sides just looking at each other; I twisted the can-pull ring around my finger of my left hand, third finger. "This had better be a temporary ring, you cheap skate, and just one other thing," I whispered, "I don't want a church, how about when we are in the states next month, it's just you and me in Las Vegas?"

Steve laughed. "I wouldn't have expected anything else from you. So you know what my next question is?"

I smiled. "I do. Baby steps, Steve, baby steps."

The End

About the Author

Joanne Rawson was born and brought up in Derbyshire England.
After leaving college in 1984, she headed off to be an au pair in the Loire Valley, France for one year. Returning back, to England, Joanne worked work for Derbyshire Education Authority in special education, and then for Derbyshire Social services working with adults with learning and physical difficulties.
In 2005, Joanne and her husband decided to give up their hectic lifestyle, after ten years of managing branded restaurants around London's M25, now spending her time in England, Goa, and Malaysia, writing romantic novels and short stories.

http://authorjoannerawson.blogspot.com/